THE GREAT RACE OF AZAMED

Kit Downes has just graduated from the University of Wales, Bangor, where he studied English and History. He spends much of his free time searching for "good" stories and writing his own when he can't find enough. The idea for *Zal and Zara and the Great Race of Azamed* came to him in a café in Hay-on-Wye the summer after leaving school, and he finished writing it in his first term at university. Kit plans to keep writing and travelling so as to avoid getting a real job for as long as possible.

First published 2008 by Walker Books Ltd
87 Vauxhall Walk, London SE11 5HJ

2 4 6 8 10 9 7 5 3 1

Text © 2008 Kit Downes
Cover illustration and chapter head illustrations © 2008 Sarah Coleman

This book has been typeset in Goudy and Byron

Printed in Great Britain by Clays Ltd, St Ives plc

British Library Cataloguing in Publication Data:
a catalogue record for this book is available from the British Library

ISBN 978-1-4063-0919-5

www.walker.co.uk

Zal and Zara and the Great Race of Azamed

KIT DOWNES

WALKER
BOOKS

Red

A spectacular dawn broke over the Great Desert. Sunlight exploded across the pale sky in a tide of glowing gold. The endless brown sand-dunes were lit up like rolling seas, captured in time and held still. The light reached Azamed, the city of flowers and carpets, making its white buildings shine.

The city was built on the sloping, ragged sides of an extinct volcano. The mountain's fiery heart was dead and cold, but the ashes provided rich soil, perfect for growing flowers in particular. Thousands of them, in myriad bright and beautiful colours, growing in gardens, pots, pools and window boxes, awoke and drank in the warm light as the new day dawned. Above the city's roofs and streets, the first few magic

carpets took to the air, gliding, rising and falling as their riders went about their business.

The Caliph Masat II of Azamed watched all of this with approval from the window of his throne room. He looked old and wizened inside his royal robes, but his mind was still sharp and quick. He cared very much for his city and its people and that morning he could tell, just by watching the sunrise, that all was right within it. He nodded his head, wrinkle-faced and white-bearded, and turned his attention back to the throne hall. This was a long white room, his golden throne at one end, the rest filled with shimmering curtains, comfortable velvet cushions and a cool bubbling fountain carved from pale pink crystal. A few proud peacocks strutted around.

Painted behind the throne was a beautiful mural of Azamed's god, the Celestial Stork, breathing the world into existence as she cried to the first dawn she saw as she flew into this universe. Now she flew eternally around the world, the beat of her wings sweeping peace and harmony and happiness down onto its people.

This morning the hall was packed with the Caliph's viziers and ministers. They were all still discussing the last item on the agenda, which had allowed the Caliph to pause to enjoy the sunrise.

The Caliph cleared his throat, careful to make it as quiet and soft as possible. Only about three of his advisers heard him, and the Caliph smiled at their frantic elbowing and kicking of their colleagues to bring them to attention.

"Now," the Caliph said. "What next?"

One of the Caliph's four Secretaries of Documents, Records and Important Lists snatched a scroll from the hands of a colleague and leapt forward to read from it. It was the Caliph's personal policy always to have at least two men doing the same job. The rivalry and suspicion this created ensured that everyone who reported to him was always absolutely truthful. If they were not, their colleagues would be quick to show them up. In Azamed's court, no bad news was dumbed down and no good news was embellished, and the Caliph always had accurate reports of what was going on.

"The next item, Your Excellency," said the secretary, "is the upcoming Great Race."

Approving murmurs ran around the throne hall. The Great Magic Carpet Race was something everyone enjoyed arguing about.

"Oh, splendid," said the Caliph, who liked the race himself. "Please begin."

Before the secretary could, one of his colleagues had snuck up behind him and snatched away the scroll. This secretary then recited what had been done in preparation for the race. Following this, one of the seven Ministers for Culture stepped forward and described the various race preparations that were still going on but would be finished by the big day. The eleven Viziers for Public Spectacles then had a brief, discreet fist fight to determine who would list what still needed to be done before the race. When the bruised winner was finished, the arguing began in earnest, with plenty of shouting, foot-stamping and colourful insults. The Caliph again found himself looking out of the window and reflecting. He loved all things about his city, but the race was by far his favourite.

The race was Azamed's greatest attraction. It was held once a year and travellers struggled across the desert to the city from all directions just to witness it. Only citizens of Azamed were allowed to compete, but that made it no less of a draw. Thousands of magic carpets, exploding out of the city and flying along an obstacle-filled track through the desert at tremendous speeds, was always a sight worth seeing. The only thing more spectacular than watching the race, the Caliph mused, was participating in it.

He had done it only once, at the age of twenty. He had disguised himself as a tax collector to ensure that anyone who might recognize him kept their distance, and had come last because of his carpet getting tangled in a palm tree. Still, despite the long hot walk back it had been one of the most fantastic days of his long life. Out over the desert was the only place where carpets could truly be flown. They were thrilling within the narrow streets and tall buildings of the city, to be sure – no one could make the zipping turns necessary to get through the market district without their heart racing. But in the Great Race, pushing your carpet to a speed that made your eyes water, with thousands of other riders trying to out-manoeuvre and overtake you, you truly felt alive.

The Caliph brought his attention back to the loudest argument, between the first Respectable Revenuer and the first Financier Bursar.

"We will need those extra seats!" One of the three Respectable Revenuers stamped his foot.

"You can't afford them!" The first Financier Bursar said, while the second held out a scroll of complicated sums.

"That's why we're asking you to pay for them!"

"We can't afford to either!"

"Yes, you can!" The third Respectable Revenuer pointed to the sheet. "You just don't want to."

"Gentlemen," said the Caliph. They all stopped in an instant and bowed to him. The Caliph motioned the fourth Vizier of the Palace Treasury to step forward.

"Would I be right in thinking that the income from the race is always quadruple the expenditure?"

The fourth vizier was a young, nervous man and he hesitated for too long, allowing the fifth, who was older and more experienced, to push him aside and step into his place.

"It has done so for the past nine hundred and ninety-nine races, Your Excellency," he said. "There is no indication that this year will be any different. Most of Azamed's hotels are already full up."

"Yes," said the Caliph. "I suspected as much.

Have the royal stables opened up for the travellers' use. Be sure to put down some fresh straw. And with regard to the extra seating the Respectable Revenuers require ..."

The revenuers' faces lit up.

"... the Financier Bursars will pay for them ..."

The bursars' faces fell.

"... and the palace will repay the bursars once the race is finished."

The whole court broke into approving, impressed murmurs. Several social climbers began clapping. Both the revenuers and bursars looked relieved, and the Caliph decided it was time for a little fun.

"Now," he said. "Who are the favourites to win this year?"

Several people tried to answer at once. A scuffle followed and the winner was the eighth Irrigation Minister.

"Opinion is divided between two candidates, Your Excellency," he said.

"And they are?" the Caliph asked.

"The Thesa family and the Shadow Society."

The Caliph knew of both, and had opinions of both, but he chose to keep them to himself.

"I see. And what has made them the favourites?"

The ninth Irrigation Minister beat his colleague to the punch.

"They are both rumoured to have woven six-coloured carpets this year, Your Excellency."

The Caliph was impressed. There was a moment of awed silence in the court, then excited talk of odds and bets began.

"Well, well," said the Caliph, sitting back on his throne. "This year's race should certainly be spectacular then."

"Yes, sir!" said the second Entertainment Minister, who was determined to be promoted to first. "It could only be more exciting if someone were to weave a rainbow carpet!"

Everyone in the throne hall burst out laughing. The third Entertainment Minister slapped his colleague on the back. A couple of the peacocks cawed. The Caliph smiled. Then one of the Catering Viziers began an argument with two of the Ministers for Foodstuffs about a missing consignment of leeks and potatoes. The Caliph shook his head and turned to sort it out.

The Caliph failed to notice, as did everyone else,

a large wicker basket at the far end of the hall. As the debate continued, the basket's lid lifted a fraction and a pair of dark eyes peeped out. The figure hiding in the basket held a large red crystal, and tapped his left fingertip against it in a fast, precise sequence. Each tap made light flash deep within the crystal, like a tiny star exploding in the night sky. No one noticed the basket, or its occupant, at all. As far as they were concerned, everything was as it should be. The race would begin in two days' time.

"The ... Thesa ... family ... and ... the ... Shado— and us!"

In the attic of a building halfway down the mountainside from the Caliph's palace, an identical red crystal lay on a table top. It was the twin of the one held by the spy in the basket, and light flashed within it at just the same time. Bhai sat before the crystal and watched the flashes without blinking. He held a sheet of parchment that showed which sequence of flashes corresponded to each letter of Azamed's alphabet, and he was translating the conversation in the throne hall as the spy relayed it to him.

"Well of course *we* are one of the favourites," said Haragan.

Both boys were fourteen and dressed from head to toe in the dark brown clothes of the Shadow Society. Brown scarves were wrapped tightly round their heads and faces. They wore gloves and even had their trouser legs tucked into their shoes. On chains round their necks they wore gold Shadow Society medallions. All that could be seen of each of them was their eyes and the bridge of the nose through the eye-slit in their scarves. Haragan had burning green eyes and Shar, watery blue. Shar was kneeling on the floor before the low table and Haragan was behind him, seated cross-legged on a magic carpet, woven of reds and oranges, that floated, rippling like lake water, in the middle of the room a few inches above the floor.

"What else are they saying?" he asked, spinning a coin between his fingers.

The Thesa family was no surprise. Haragan had known he would have to face them since the proud day when he had been commanded to win the Great Race for the Society.

He did not intend to fail.

The Shadow Society had been founded nearly a thousand years ago by near-legendary and much venerated Salladan Shadow: magician, soldier, intriguer and prophet. To him it had been revealed that the legend of the Celestial Stork was nothing but camelpat. The real creator was the Cosmos Vulture, the last survivor of an older universe. Picking the meat from the bones of the ancient gods, the vulture had acquired their power to create substance from nothingness. Obligated to use the power he had obtained, the Cosmos Vulture had created the new universe and everything within it. Now he flew around the world each day; night came when his wings passed in front of the sun. He looked down on the people he had created and judged how well they were using the gifts he had given them.

The Shadow Society believed in using everything the Cosmos Vulture had given them to the full. They led lives dedicated to self-improvement – physical exercise, scholarship, the fulfilment of potential and the overcoming of obstacles – all for the glory of the Cosmos Vulture, who would reward those who did not take his blessing for granted but strived to aid themselves. The most faithful were permitted to ride upon his wings in the next life.

Part of the Society's necessary discipline was secrecy. It had to be kept pure from the poisonous influence of everyday Azamed, or its members might become lax and lazy. The members of the Society (no one knew how many there were, as most were brought in at birth) hid in broad daylight. They never ventured from their secret headquarters without their protective brown clothes and scarves. All they desired and all they strove for was the blessing of the Cosmos Vulture and the continued glory of the Society – although not necessarily in that order. Most members saw nothing wrong with a little moderate breaking of the Caliph's laws. He did worship the false Celestial Stork after all.

Haragan was as dedicated to the creed as any of the Society's teenage acolytes. His muscles still ached from his morning fitness training, a sign he was doing it well.

"The Thesas..." translated Shar. "They ... they have ... a six-coloured carpet!"

Haragan's head shot up.

That meant only one thing.

She was helping them. It was the one possible

explanation. There were too few people in Azamed capable of it. The Thesas were the only team she had reason to help. And who else would they ask? Beneath his scarf, Haragan's face twisted into an ugly grimace. It showed in his eyes and made Shar nervous enough to lean away from him.

She never seemed to be satisfied. *She* always came back to bite him again. Her hunger for his failure seemed to be insatiable...

He began to calm down. Getting angry would not help. Discipline was everything to the Society's members; to Haragan, it was one step removed from food. In fact, the news changed very little. *She* would not beat him.

"A six-colour carpet?" he said to Shar, a plan already forming.

"That's what they said." Shar's voice was muffled. He was new to the Society, sent to Haragan for mentoring, and was not yet used to speaking with half a mouthful of scarf. "Six colours. Just like ours. They're going to be the biggest competition."

"No," said Haragan, holding up a gloved finger. "What does one do to a disadvantage?"

The question was an ancient piece of Shadow

Society doctrine, and Shar's answer was perfect.

"Eliminate it," he said. "Do all you can to achieve victory before any game begins."

"And the race is no different," said Haragan. His plan was formed in his mind. "The Thesas have a six-colour. That *could* have made them our biggest competition…"

"But it isn't going to?" Shar suggested.

"Correct." Haragan smiled behind his scarf.

She would not beat him.

Orange

Zal Thesa stood in his garden and practised. It was the family garden, but so early in the morning, when he was the only one awake, he felt as if it belonged to him and him alone. It was a small and very private garden, with a high stone wall all the way round it. There were no plants, just fresh green grass and a tall, twisting apple tree, which grew beside a small silvery pond. Zal stood beneath the tree, utter concentration on his face. In his left hand was his sword; in his right, seven silk hand-kerchiefs, each a different colour. He held the sword's wooden grip tightly so it would neither slip nor rub. Zal slowed his breathing and tried to concentrate harder. He had spent an hour last night sharpening and polishing his sword, and the curved blade gleamed like snow at sunrise. He shifted his feet on the damp grass. His knees felt tense, so he relaxed them and did the same for his elbows. He wouldn't get anywhere unless he relaxed. He breathed out, and could wait no longer.

Zal threw the handkerchiefs high up into the air. The bundle separated, and all the colours of the rainbow filled his vision as they descended. They fell, twisting and rippling. Quick as lightning, Zal swung the sword up and began to cut back and forth in the air. He moved so fast, his arm became a blur. The sunlight flashed and exploded up and down the moving blade. This was the seven-colours test; a test of swordsmanship that required the utmost skill to pass. The aim was cut all seven handkerchiefs in half before they fell to the earth. Zal slowed his arm and came to a stop. His muscles were burning. His sword had seemed lighter than a feather at the start of the exercise, and now felt as heavy as lead. He breathed deep and slow again, drawing air into his dry lungs, and looked down at his feet.

All seven handkerchiefs lay there intact. For the

ninth time that morning, he had missed every single one of them.

"Curses!" Zal spun on his heel and kicked the tree trunk. His little dog, Rip, who was dozing at the foot of the tree, opened his eyes to discover that the blue handkerchief had fallen onto his nose. He shook it off and stood up on his paws, yapping in indignation. Zal was too angry to listen.

Why couldn't he do it? He could cut one falling handkerchief without even having to think about it. Two, he had only to glance at. Three, he had to glance and blink once, and so on, up to six falling handkerchiefs, all of which he could cut in half, or even into thirds. But seven! Seven somehow eluded him, and he couldn't understand why. No matter how hard he practised, it still eluded him, and this was the third morning he had tried seven, and still…

"Still no luck?"

Zal looked up and realized, to his horror, that he was still standing on one foot. He put his other foot down and straightened up.

"No, not yet," he replied.

Zara Aura was standing at the top of the steps to the house and she was, as usual, the last person Zal wanted to see. The opposite was true for Rip, who scampered forward, yelping with joy. Zara crouched down and scratched behind his long floppy ears, causing him to roll about in ecstasy.

"Would you please not do that!" Zal said in exasperation. "It isn't making him the kind of fighting dog I'm going to need."

"He's never going to be the kind of fighting dog you think you're going to need," replied Zara as she carried on scratching. "You should be content with the dog you've got. And he's just adorable."

They glowered at each other. Zal was thin and wiry but strong. His face was pleasant when he wasn't scowling, and his light brown hair swept forward into a cocky crest. Zara was slim too but feminine with it – a little shorter than Zal, with blonde hair that came to just below her ears. They were both twelve and had been engaged to be married for six years now. Their two fathers had seen nothing but good in an alliance between the Thesa and Aura families. The children had disagreed, and time had done nothing to lessen the mutual contempt Zal and Zara felt for each other.

"Are you here for any reason," Zal said, "other

than to mock me?" He turned away and began col-
lecting up the handkerchiefs.

"Would I come out here willingly?" Zara said.
"Your father wants you in the workshop. You need to
finish the racing carpet."

"What? I finished weaving it yesterday evening."

Zal had devoted an hour to the carpet after dinner the night before. He didn't like carpet-weaving
and so always worked fast in order to finish as soon
as possible. The consequence of this was that he had
become by far the fastest carpet-weaver in Azamed.

"All that needs doing is for the magic to be put
in," he said.

"Yes. That's what I'm here for," said Zara, who
was one of the few children to be born in Azamed
each year with the gift of magic. She attended the
school of Azamed's Guild of Magicians and was
halfway through her time there.

"Then what do I need to come in for?" said Zal.
"I've got practice to do."

Zal had no interest in becoming a carpet-weaver
once he grew up. The fact that the last eighteen
generations of the Thesa family had been weavers
meant little to him. His ambition was to join the

Caliph's Citadel Guard – the fearless soldiers who policed the streets of Azamed having daring, hair-raising adventures by the day. To that end, Zal spent three hours every morning practising swordsmanship.

"I don't particularly want you there either," said Zara. "But *they* do. So come on."

"Oh, I don't believe this!"

Zal pushed his sword back into its scabbard, making the metal shriek. Zara stood up and walked back into the house with Rip in her arms, Zal stomping up the steps behind her. The Thesa house was large but plain, with just a few pieces of furniture and decoration to make it a home. Its greatest feature was the patchwork of dozens of multicoloured carpets spread across the floors and stairs, making it very uneven underfoot. They passed through the kitchen and sitting room and into the large workroom behind the shop where the carpets were sold. Zal's father, Augur Thesa, and Zara's father, Arna Aura, were waiting for them.

"Ah! There you are!" boomed Arna, slapping his hands to the sides of his large, round stomach.

"Hello, Mr Aura," said Zal. "Dad. Do you really need me here for this?"

It was obvious that Augur was expecting this, and had prepared for it, but he made a very good show of looking shocked.

"Zal! This is your carpet! Of course you need to be here! You've been working at it for weeks."

"Yes," said Zal, trying to sound patient and reasonable. "But I finished it last night."

The carpet in question was stretched out on the floor between the parents and the children. It was a rectangle (no other shape could be made to fly), about ten feet long and five feet wide, and was woven with clear patterns which Zal had taken some time over, just to please his father. It contained six colours: blue, red, yellow, violet, green and orange.

"Zal," repeated Augur, "this is your carpet. You should be there at every stage in its weaving. The enchanting is the most important part. What is a carpet without an enchantment? It is nothing more than a rug. Of course you need to be here."

"But there's nothing for me to do!" Zal said.

"Well, no," said Augur, "except watch how the magic flows through your knots to see how you can improve them on your next carpet."

"Oh, come on!"

"You're also here to provide moral support to your future wife," suggested Arna.

"WE ARE NOT GETTING MARRIED!"

Zal and Zara yelled so loudly that everything in the room seemed to flinch. Rip jumped in the air, barking. Both fathers recoiled and tried to hide behind each other. Zal and Zara simmered and trembled like boiling cooking pots.

"All right. All right. It's OK," said Augur.

"Yes! Yes!" said Arna. "It's fine."

There was a moment's pause.

"You're not getting married," Arna said. "Just yet."

"NO!" they exploded again.

"Not now!"

"Not ever!"

"NO!"

Both parents remained hopeful that the eventual marriage would be a success. Augur and Arna were very much family men, but both were widowers and they were keen to ensure that their children were successful in life. Marrying Zara's magical talents to Zal's weaving ability would produce a formidable duo in the carpet business.

"Fine," said Augur from behind Arna. "We'll say no more about it. Zara, perhaps you should start?"

Zara gave her father another ferocious look and then nodded.

"I'm going to carry on practising," said Zal in a voice that defied anyone to challenge him. He stalked to an empty space at the end of the workroom, between two racks of threads. He drew his scimitar with a flourish and began a slow sword fight with an imaginary opponent.

Zara shook her head and sat down on the floor at one end of the racing carpet, cross-legged with her back to Zal and their fathers, who watched over her shoulders. She gazed at the carpet. Despite his indifferent attitude, Zal *had* put some effort into it. The sequence of colours had been well thought out.

Magic worked in colours, and there were seven – the same as appeared in a rainbow. Each had its own strengths and weaknesses; Zal's choices would make this carpet a very fine one. The red would carry energy through it. The yellow would balance it in the air, riding it along the beams of sunlight. The violet would let it touch the air all around it, not just fly through. The blue would keep it steady in rain and storms. Green would give it power over the greatest enemy: gravity. Orange would give it a tremendous burst of speed. The carpet would never be able to accelerate quite as fast as if indigo had been included, but it would be far steadier when it reached its top speed.

Overall, the combination was excellent. Six-colour carpets were easy to weave but hard to enchant: there were too few magicians who could wield six colours, let alone manipulate them all at once to fill a carpet with magic. Zara, who had been born with all seven colours of magic within her, found it easy. Arna had often remarked that it was a shame seven-colour carpets were impossible.

"Light the incense, please."

Augur lit a long taper from an oil lamp and carried it over to an incense-burner. Thin blue smoke that smelled of dried flowers and mountain forests was soon drifting from it and dissipating around the room, clearing Zara's head and helping her to both relax and concentrate. Behind them, Zal mimed a parry; the only sounds were the muffled movements of his clothing. Zara stretched out her hands, spreading her fingers, and placed them along the tasselled edge of the carpet. Rip trotted round her, panting with excitement.

Zara took a slow, deep breath and began. Her magic came alive, the way a fireplace smoulders, then bursts into life. Magic flowed through her fingertips and into the carpet like warm water. It flooded through the threads, spiralling and weaving along the lines and patterns. The colours, which had been plain and ordinary, became vibrant, shining and sparkling with magic. The transformation raced from one end of the carpet to the other as the dawn light had raced across the desert, pushing back the night's darkness. It reached the end, trembling along the tassels, and then the carpet lifted off the floor, rising several inches into the air. Rip yipped with excitement. Augur and Arna gasped and clapped their hands. The carpet shuddered, steadied and floated evenly in the air.

"Splendid! Wondrous!" Arna ruffled Zara's hair as he laughed.

"Excellent! Absolute excellence. From both of you ... Zal!"

Zal cut down his phantom enemy and turned to look at the carpet for the first time.

"Very nice," he said and raised his scimitar again. Zara sighed with irritation and resumed scratching Rip.

"You made it," said Augur. "You two together. And you did it very well."

"Thank you," said Zal, slashing the air. "Can I go now?"

Augur looked aghast.

"Zal! You're going to be racing on it—"

"What?" Zal spun round. "We had a deal. I wove the racing carpet and I could have my sword sharpened by a proper blacksmith. We never said anything about me racing on it."

"You don't want to?" asked his father.

"No!" said Zal firmly.

"Well, whoever's riding it, I want to be co-pilot," said Zara. "It wouldn't be off the ground without me." She stepped onto the floating carpet. It rippled, but supported her. She sat down on it, cross-legged. Rip hopped on and off beside her, yapping in delight.

"Come along, Zal. You wove it, so you should ride it."

"It is, after all, the Great Race..." said Arna.

"*The race!*" Zal exploded angrily. "It's all anyone talks about for weeks before and months after. It's like the most important thing in the universe. I'm sick and tired of going through *the race* every year."

"Zal," said Augur. "You're twelve. You're eligible to race. Our family have been competing ..."

"... in an unbroken line for seventeen generations and you've done it every year since you were twelve," Zal recited. "That's another thing I'm sick and tired of: our ancestors and all their heroics on carpets. But I don't want to be a weaver or a racer. I want to be a guardsman. Is that really so bad?"

"No, of course it isn't," said Augur. "It's a respectable career, sometimes prestigious. But..."

"You've won seven times," said Zal. "Try and make it eight while I practise the skills I'm going to need for what *I* want to do."

"All right," said Augur. "If you don't want to race, I won't force you."

"Nothing will make me compete in the race."

With that, Zal sheathed his scimitar and marched, guardsman-like, out of the room. Rip jumped down from the hovering carpet and chased after his master. Arna sighed with relief and Augur sighed with sadness.

"Dad," said Zara, "I need to get on with my homework."

"Of course, my dear. Go ahead," said her father.

As Zara stepped off the carpet, it drifted lazily back down to the floor like a falling leaf. She went through to the kitchen.

"Now, don't lose heart, my friend." Arna placed a comforting hand on Augur's shoulder. "He is twelve. He's meant to be angry and rebellious."

"Yes, I know," said Augur. "He doesn't understand how special magic carpets are. Do you know, there are lands where they're nothing more than legends? It's such a shame he doesn't realize his own talent. Certainly he's a fine swordsman, but he can weave faster than anyone I have ever seen. He always contents himself with the minimum of effort; if he tried, his work could be wondrous. And of course, I apologize for the insults he continues to heap on your daughter."

"That is unnecessary. She heaps almost the same amount on him! Maybe you will have to be the racer again this year, but I'm sure your son will be happy for you if you win. And Zara will not let either of you down. Who knows, he might yet change his mind."

"No," said Zal, coming back in. He had returned to collect his seven handkerchiefs. "Nothing – *nothing* – will make me compete in the race."

Night had fallen and Azamed lay sleeping. The sky was black and dusted with countless stars. A crescent moon glowed down on the city. The streets were empty, all the shops shut up for the night. Everything was still.

A grappling hook, wrapped in cloth to make no sound, flew through the air and hooked over the Thesas' garden wall. Shar's head peered over a few seconds later. He looked around, then clambered up.

He dropped onto the grass in near silence and then crept up to the apple tree, moving like a cat. Producing a small wooden whistle from a hidden pocket, Shar raised it to his lips and blew three notes: an almost perfect impression of a desert owl's mating call. Haragan climbed over the wall and joined him by the tree. Four more Shadow Society members followed, each laden with climbing tools and weapons beneath their disguises. They hurried up to the house, their feet making little noise on the grass and none on the steps. One of the four, Dari, crouched on the top step and drew out some long, slender lock-picking tools.

Haragan stood behind Dari as he fiddled and tweaked at the door lock, and looked around him in distaste. It was a nice garden. In his mind's eye, Haragan could see children playing and laughing within its walls: running round the tree, peeping into the pond and scrambling up the ivy on the wall. Doing all the things children were meant to do with their endless hours. It was a long way removed from the childhood he'd enjoyed – but that did not matter. *She* and her Thesa boyfriend might have had the idyllic upbringing, but he was about to have the last laugh.

Haragan had been certain that he would enjoy this from the moment he had come up with the idea. It would be more fun than when he had stolen the hair from the nineteenth Medicine Minister's head and taken his eyebrows for good measure. It was already more thrilling than breaking into Azamed's revenue building to put paper-eating beetles in with the records of all the taxes the Shadow Society had evaded. And while it wasn't as dangerous as kidnapping one hundred and fifty children at once, a feat of which he had been particularly proud, it was far more devious. By the time Dari had got the lock undone, Haragan was grinning.

Upstairs, Zal was dreaming.

"Do you, Zal Thesa, take this woman as your wife?"

"I d—"

"AAARGH!" Zal sat bolt upright in bed, almost tearing the blanket with his clenched hands. Rip, who had been sleeping curled at the foot of the bed, looked up and gave a tired, groggy yip.

"Sorry, sorry," said Zal. "Just a dream. A horrible, horrible dream."

He got out of bed, still in his nightgown, to get a glass of water. Rip yapped again, raised himself on his tired, unsteady paws and followed.

"No. No, boy. It's not morning yet."

"Wruff!"

"Oh, all right." Zal gave up and let Rip follow him in the darkness down the corridor to the bathroom. They were halfway there, just passing the door of the first spare bedroom, when two strange noises came from downstairs. The first was Dari tripping over a chair in the workroom and just managing to catch it before it toppled over. The second was Haragan slapping Dari across the back of the head and causing him to drop the chair anyway. It landed with a loud, clattering crash.

Zal stood, trying to decide if he'd imagined the sounds. The door to the spare room opened, revealing Zara.

"AAARGH!" Zal screamed for a second time. Zara's sudden appearance and white nightgown had made him think for a moment that his dream had come true. What had actually happened was that Augur and Arna had been up late into the evening reviewing their carpet orders for the next six months: Augur had invited Arna and Zara to spend the night to save them the long walk home. Zal, who had been sulking in the garden at Zara's continued presence throughout the day, had missed the invitation.

"What are *you* doing here?"

"What are *you* playing at?" Zara said. "What's all the noise?"

"You heard it too?"

Rip, now wide awake, began growling.

Downstairs, the Shadow Society realized they had been discovered. All thoughts of stealth were forgotten and they rushed about their tasks.

Hearing them, Zal and Zara made their decision without speaking. Zal snatched up his sword, which had been resting close to hand on a side table. Zara picked up an oil lamp and ignited it with a whisper of magic. The pair then hurried downstairs side by side and gasped in horror as they rushed into the workroom.

Their six-colour racing carpet had been cut into small, ragged pieces. Every other carpet in the workroom, and through into the shop, had been destroyed – slashed with sharp daggers. All of the unfinished carpets, spare wool and weaving tools had been piled up in the middle of the room and doused with oil, ready to be burned. The six Shadow Society members were frozen in their positions as Zal and Zara looked around in horror, and not without a little bemusement. Shadow Society procedure taught that when a disguise was necessary, a bizarre one was best. If a Shadow dressed as a slipper-maker committed fraud, burglary or vandalism, the Guard would begin their search for the culprit at the Guild of Slipper-Makers. But if the Shadow did it dressed in a wolf costume, the Guard would have a harder time finding somewhere to start. Zal and Zara were confronted by six figures dressed as the Celestial Stork, the Cosmos Vulture and four of Azamed's minor gods: the Spring Sparrow, the Forest Flamingo, the River Robin and the Precipice Pelican.

Then Zara's eyes met with one of them. "Haragan!" Her horror changed into furious rage.

Haragan moved as fast as a cobra. A jet of blue magic shot from his hand and flew at Zara's face. She summoned a strange red light into her right palm and knocked the blue aside with it, using her left hand to send a green jet back at him. Rip launched himself forward and sunk his teeth into Shar's feather-covered leg. Dari and the other three drew large curved daggers from under their wings and charged at Zal.

Zal's scimitar was out of its scabbard before they'd crossed half the distance. He spun, jumped and ducked, fighting off all four at once. Their blades scraped and clashed together. White sparks and severed feathers flew, mixing with the storm of magic being exchanged between Zara and Haragan. Bolts and jets of all colours flew and deflected, burning holes in the floor and ceiling. Zara ground her teeth, her face locked in a scowl. Haragan! How dare he? How dare he do this! Of all their previous encounters, of every dirty trick he had ever concocted, this was the worst! But she couldn't allow herself to get too angry. That would damage her concentration and give him the edge. She put more energy into her next bolt and it came very close to breaking his defences.

Haragan, too, was furious. *She* was here! How could he not have thought of it? He'd known she was engaged to the Thesa heir. The wedding was years away, but why hadn't he thought of it? Why hadn't he planned for the possibility? Here *she* was again, with *her* cruel luck, taking his careful, brilliant plans and tearing them asunder. How dare she. *She* would not win! He pressed his magic home with renewed vigour.

Zal sidestepped one dagger, kicked a Shadow's leg out from under him, parried another dagger and then brought his blade back to slash the wielder's wrist. He was at first filled with raw, burning fury.

His home had been invaded and his father's carpets destroyed. He would make them suffer for it all. But his training was paying off. He was controlling his anger and fighting with skill and precision. His enemies were falling back, becoming more cautious as they saw his real talent. A couple of them were even becoming afraid! Zal was starting to enjoy himself. *This* was what he'd been up practising for every morning since he was eight. *This* was what the Citadel Guard was really about. *This* would look good when it was written on his application form.

Then a dagger passed close to his face and, with a jolt, Zal recognized it. It was a Burying Blade – all the daggers were, he realized. When Burying Blades were forged, very dark, very evil magic was poured into the metal. They were never, ever used to practise with. They were weapons that could only be used once. When they were thrust into something they would bury themselves, digging their blade in up to the hilt, sometimes further. Once in, they could never be removed. Eventually, inevitably, they killed – but caused constant, indescribable pain for the victim, who would have to live out their last few days with the dagger lodged in their flesh.

With a new concern for his own, and Zara's, safety, Zal concentrated on parrying and attacking his enemy's knife hands. But grim pleasure still rode through him as he fought. Sounds of movement and the voices of Augur and Arna came from upstairs.

Suddenly Shar, who had been dancing around trying to shake off Rip, collided with Dari. As the two of them toppled to the floor, Dari dropped his knife. There was a drilling, creaking sound and a jet of fine sawdust flew up into the air as it buried itself up to the hilt in the floorboards. At the same moment Zara hit Haragan with a low-power spell and sent him staggering. As he tripped over the dagger hilt and fell backwards, a bolt shot from his failing hand and ignited the oil on the pile of tools and carpet materials. A column of fire roared up in the middle of the room. Shar and Dari rolled out of the way and Rip rushed behind Zal and Zara, who were stumbling back from the wave of heat, half blinded by the sudden light in the dark room.

"Let's go!" Haragan yelled. Ducking round the fire and back through the house, the Shadow Society members disappeared out into the night.

Guided by Rip's anxious barking, Zal and Zara

made it back to the door by the stairs just as Augur and Arna appeared and saw the blaze. As the two fathers yelled and screamed, Zara summoned her magic. The smoke that was filling the room suddenly changed into a fluffy grey cloud. Rain poured down from it, extinguishing the flames and drumming on the floorboards. Lightning flashed a few times and then dissipated, leaving the workroom filled with nothing but wet ashes and steam.

Everyone began to breathe again as the air cooled.

"What on earth has been going on?" said Augur.

Yellow

It was the next morning. Augur, Arna and Zara, who had taken the day off school, were standing in the ruined shopfront, telling the story to Captain Burs of the Caliph's Citadel Guard. Everything had been blackened by the flames and then drenched by Zara's rainstorm. The shop was now damp and chilly and the cold air smelt of charcoal.

"And you're certain they were members of the Shadow Society?" said Captain Burs.

"For the third time, *yes*," said Zara, but Arna waved her to silence.

"Yes, Captain," said Augur. "She and my son saw them at very close quarters."

"And I recognized Haragan," said Zara.

"Even with his mask. I know it was him."

"I see," said the captain. "But you have no evidence at all?"

"No," said Augur, anger slipping into his usually calm voice. "Once the fire was out, there didn't seem to be much else we could do until morning, so we all went back to bed. That was a mistake. We didn't realize that they'd used oil from my own lamps to start the fire..."

"Which is why it looks like it was started by accident?" said Burs.

"Yes. And at some time in the night they must have come back and taken the floorboard with the dagger in it."

"And pulled up the ones on either side to make it look like it had been burned up," Burs added.

"Yes."

"Look, we are *not* making this up!" Zara said. "It happened! It was the Shadow Society..."

"Zara!"

"Miss Aura, I believe you," said Captain Burs. "If the fire had burned long and hot enough to consume three floorboards, there should be a lot more damage than there is. But that isn't enough. I need more evidence than that before I can even go near the Shadow Society. But I do believe you. This is just the kind of dirty trick they would sink to if they wanted to win the Great Race. They've done it to me before."

"To you?" said Augur.

"Several times I've come close to being able to arrest Shadow Society members," said Burs. "But each time, the evidence has vanished at the crucial moment and I've ended up being humiliated in court. I've lost three of their headscarves, numerous weapons, a whole file of incriminating documents and a live zebra. Each item could have sent a Shadow to prison, but they were too quick."

"But I know it was Haragan!" Zara cried. "Even though he was dressed as a bird. Get someone to put a truth spell on me and you'll see."

"Even that won't help, Miss Aura," said Burs. "Truth spells are too easily discredited in court. I'll tell you what will happen if I do approach them – I know from long experience. I'll tell the leader his men are suspected of burglary and arson. He'll ask to see what evidence I've got. When I have nothing, he'll write immediately to the Caliph, claiming that

I am unfairly persecuting the Society for no other reason than that I think the Cosmos Vulture is a false god. The Caliph will then summon me and ask for an explanation. He will listen to my theories, but he'll also ask to see evidence. When I have nothing, he'll order me to back down to avoid offending the Society any further."

"So there's nothing you can do?" said Zara.

"Unless you can find something that proves they were here, then no," said Burs. "But I will add this incident to my file on them. If it gets big enough, the Caliph might give me permission for a full investigation of the Society without evidence. But I'm afraid it won't happen soon."

At that moment, a carrier pigeon fluttered into the shop and landed on Burs' shoulder. It carried a message summoning him to another case. He apologized again and left.

"Curse the Shadow Society!" said Arna. "They're like venomous snakes in Azamed's garden. If you step on one, even by accident, it bites you. Then all of its friends crawl out of the thistles to bite as well. And none of your friends can help because you're surrounded by biting snakes. Curse them all!"

Augur looked around his ruined shop.

"Zal was right," he said. "We do make the race far too important if this is how far people are prepared to go to win."

"Now, don't lose heart, friend," said Arna. "There is always next year."

"I'm afraid there may not be," Augur said.

"What? Oh, come now. Even the Shadows can't prevent the changing of the seasons. At least I hope not."

"No," said Augur, "that's not what I meant. I've only got myself to blame. I spent far more money than I should have on the materials for the racing carpet. Even if we didn't win, we were guaranteed second or third place with it. That would have brought in much business for the shop, and I was sure I'd remake the money fast. But now I can't enter the race. I have no carpets to sell, and no materials to make them, and no money to buy new materials. I'm ruined."

"Holy Stork!" said Arna. "I had no idea."

"Of course you didn't. It is all my own fault."

"But you must have some savings…?"

"I do. Just about enough to feed Zal and myself for

a few months. But not enough to start the business going again."

"Oh dear," said Arna. "Well, let's not panic. If you aren't going to starve right now, that gives us some time. We'll come up with something."

"We need to get back in the race," said Zara.

Both men looked at her, wide-eyed.

"The prize money," she said. "Ten thousand gold pieces. It'll be more than enough to—"

"Zara, the race is off for us," said her father.

"OFF?" Zara looked at them in disbelief. "We're just going to let them get away with it? They do all this, and we're just going to let them win?"

"Think straight!" Arna said. "If we weave a new carpet, they'll just come back to destroy it again. And Stork knows how much more damage they can do."

"I thanked the Celestial Stork this morning that the house is still standing," said Augur. "I won't do anything that could provoke the Shadows further. I can't lose anything else. No, we are not weaving a new carpet."

"I'm sorry, Zara," Arna said, "but the Shadow Society has won."

Zara glared at them both with pure fury. There

was a moment of silence.

"Well, you two can give up," she said. "But we're going to do something."

She marched out of the room and stomped up the stairs.

"*We?*" said Arna.

In a dark room in a secret part of Azamed, a meeting was taking place. Haragan stood to attention. Shar and Dari stood behind him. Before them, the Leader of the Shadow Society reclined on a large cushion. His face was also hidden in a scarf.

Haragan was not thrilled that the master had summoned them. The mission was over. They'd succeeded. He had been planning a nice relaxing day of racing practice, and instead he had to dance on ceremony. Also, anyone who went near the master – other than his bodyguards – was searched for weapons. The two female bodyguards (the only women allowed in the Shadow Society, a role they had inherited from their mothers) had found all of Haragan's, even his secret ones, leaving him feeling naked and nervous. And he did not like the current leader. In the early days of the Society, Salladan

Shadow had picked his greatest pupil to replace him, his greatest pupil had picked his greatest pupil, and so on. According to the Society's code, a member should be prepared to lay down his life for his leader. But Haragan would have had difficulty doing that for the man who had sent him in *there*.

"So," said the Leader, who liked to think he reminded his underlings of a sleepy tiger: relaxed, but still very dangerous. "The Thesas discovered you in the act, did they?"

"It was unfortunate, Master," said Haragan, who thought of the Leader as a lazy sloucher who was not half as clever as he thought he was. "I hadn't counted on the dog being awake so late at night."

Before they'd been shown in, Haragan had threatened Shar and Dari with dire consequences at the merest mention of the chair.

"Hmmph," said the Leader. "Too few of the lesser animals respect the glorious Cosmos Vulture's desire for them to sleep when his wings cover the sun."

"But it was a tiny setback," Haragan added. "We'd already completed the two biggest parts of the plan when they arrived."

"You destroyed their racing carpet and all their

materials?" The Leader played with the tassel on the corner of a cushion with his gloved fingers. Haragan could not tell if it was from boredom or a nervous twitch.

"We destroyed all their carpets, Master. They won't be competing in the race."

"Good ... good," said the Leader. "And how is *our* racing carpet progressing?"

Haragan also did not like how the Leader had the audience chamber decorated. Gold and jewelled trinkets, worth whole fortunes, glistened and sparkled from every surface. It was not a statement of wealth, but a test. While the Shadows were often thieves, they stole with discipline. They resisted theft for personal greed or vanity and only stole when the whole Society could benefit from it and when the glory of the Cosmos Vulture demanded it. They had to prove this by ignoring the Leader's collection, showing it was not a temptation. It was a silly, tedious test in Haragan's eyes. The punishment for theft from the Society was enough on its own: the cutting off of the fingers you had used.

"It is finished," answered Haragan. He was irked that the Leader could call it "our" when he had contributed nothing to its weaving. "I added the magic when we returned. We are ready to race."

"Hmm," said the Leader. "But Zara Aura recognized you?"

"No, Master," said Haragan, who was prepared for this. "She merely assumed it was me."

"But she assumed correctly?"

"Yes, but it was still a guess."

A silence followed, and Haragan realized he had just contradicted the Leader. A distant corner of his mind began to weigh up the merits of each of his fingers, choosing which could be offered to the knife.

"Hmm," said the Leader again. "I would have expected you, Haragan, to be the last person to underestimate her. Considering your history."

"Yes, Master." Haragan looked at the floor.

"Perhaps this is a message," the Leader said. "Perhaps the glorious Cosmos Vulture wishes you to spend another day in the Dark Room. To refresh your memory."

A tremor ran through Haragan from head to toe. The mere name of *there* refreshed his memory. Pictures flashed across his eyes. Screams, shrieks and terrible moans echoed in his ears. His hands ached for his weapons, then to clench into fists, but he kept them still at his side.

"Perhaps, Master." He let not one hint of his feelings show. Even behind the mask, behind the expressionless eyes, he could read his Leader's disappointment.

"But as you completed the mission, and there is nothing either family can do about it, I suppose there is not much point."

"No, Master."

"Carry on, Haragan. All glory to the Cosmos Vulture."

"Thank you, Master. Eternal glory to the Cosmos Vulture."

"Dismissed. All power, splendour and grandeur to the Cosmos Vulture for ever!"

The three young Shadows bowed and walked backwards out of the room. Haragan would normally have remembered not to bother trying to outdo the Leader in praising the Cosmos Vulture. But he was too busy fuming.

"That seemed OK," said Dari once they were in the corridor.

"Don't be ridiculous," said Haragan. "He's nowhere near satisfied. Come on."

He led them briskly down the corridor.

"Where are we going?" Shar asked, jogging to keep up.

"Back to the Thesas'. To double-check there are no clues left."

Zara found Zal in his bedroom, pulling on his armour. It was made of light-brown leather and was covered in scratches from fencing competitions. Zal was fumbling with the straps and buckles as he tried to do them up too fast, hissing curses under his breath.

"Zal, what are you doing?"

"I'm going to get them," he said, not looking up.

"Get them?"

"I am going to find those filthy camelpats and cut them into more pieces than our carpet."

Zara started at his ferocity. "You're declaring a vendetta against the Shadow Society?"

"Yes," he said. He finished with the last strap and pushed his sheathed sword through his belt. "I'm going to hunt down every single stinking one of them and make them pay for last night!"

He pushed Zara aside and strode down the stairs. Rip padded along beside him, growling in anticipation. Zara followed and grabbed his arm.

"This isn't a good idea. In fact, it's a stupid idea."

"Oh, and do you have a better one?" Zal twisted free and continued through the house. "Our wise fathers do. Give up. Sit back and let them do this to us. Over my dead body!"

"If you do this, the race will happen over your dead body," said Zara, who had heard the rumours of what befell those who offended the Shadow Society. "You'll be in some shallow grave out in the sands!"

"I'm not trying to stop them being in the stupid race. I don't care about the race!" Zal shouted. "Though now you mention it, I'll wreck their racing carpet while I'm at it. They invaded my home and nearly destroyed it. It's a matter of honour!"

"Zal! They'll kill you." Zara grabbed him again as he walked down the steps into the garden and towards the back gate.

"They can try!"

"Zal! The Shadows have hundreds of men. You can't take them all on single-handed!"

"I'm going—"

Zara pushed him into the pond.

It was much deeper than either of them had realized, full of weeds and slime and very cold. Zal plunged in feet first and vanished under the water. He erupted, spluttering, a second later, drenched to the skin. He looked at Zara in disbelief. There was a moment's pause as they glared at one another.

"What did you do that for?" Zal shouted.

"To cool you down," said Zara, offering him her hand. "Come on."

Zal tried twice to haul himself out, but slipped back each time. Scowling, he took her hand. Zara dug in her heels and pulled him, splashing and dripping, out onto the grass.

"Now," said Zara, "you are *not* going to war with the Shadows."

"You're wrong," said Zal. "I still am – and getting me wet is not going to stop me!"

He turned and began to walk away. Zara rolled her eyes and then snapped her fingers. The ground suddenly came alive. It rippled upwards in small thick waves of grass and soil, each a foot high, which broke over Zal's feet, burying them.

"Hey!" Zal waved his arms for balance, toppled forward and landed in press-up position.

"Let me go!" He grabbed his ankles and tugged, but Zara clenched her fist and the magic in the soil tightened its grip. Two of the apple tree's roots wove forward to wrap round Zal's ankles.

"Not until you listen to me," said Zara. "Your father has lost everything else. He doesn't need to lose his son too."

Zal stopped. He twisted his head round to look at her.

"What?"

Zara knelt down beside him and explained how all the Thesa capital had gone into the racing carpet, and that with the workshop gone, there was little chance of regaining it. Zal's face grew paler and his expression more horrified.

"What are we going to do?" he finally murmured.

"Well, I've got a better solution than throwing yourself at Haragan's knives," said Zara. "We need to weave a new carpet and compete in the race – and we need to win."

"What? How is that a solution?" exclaimed Zal. "We have no materials and no money!"

"We'll pick them up on the way," said Zara. She muttered a few magic words and the earth relaxed. Zal quickly rolled free and shook the earth from his shoes.

"But what are you talking about?" he demanded. "We can't weave a carpet in a day and a night. No one can!"

"Let's cross that bridge when we come to it," said Zara. "What we need to do first of all is guarantee that we're going to win."

"You…"

"That's right," she said. "We need to find out how to weave a rainbow carpet!"

"Rainbow carpet?" said Zal. "A rainbow carpet! You need a doctor. Rainbow carpets are what the Blue Caliph rides around on in stories and songs. They can't really be made. This is a worse idea than mine!"

"Thanks for admitting that yours was bad," said Zara, "but you're wrong. They can be woven. Come on, I'll prove it to you."

Zara started towards the gate, but Zal stayed where he was and crossed his arms. Rip, who had begun to follow Zara, looked uneasily back and forth between them.

"I'm not going anywhere," Zal said. "I need to talk to Dad, work out what we're—"

"You said yourself, he wants to give up," Zara interrupted. "And yes, you *are* coming. Come on."

"No, I'm… Hey! What the…? Stop!" Zal cried as his legs suddenly moved of their own accord, carrying him towards Zara in a stumbling walk. Without any intention on his part, his feet rose, moved forward and fell back to the ground – and no matter how he strained and wrenched his muscles, he could not stop them.

"Just a joint-control spell," said Zara. "Just move with it and you won't feel any pain."

"No! Stop! Let me go!" Zal shouted as Zara ran through the gate and he began reluctantly to run after her. Rip barked with delight and followed.

Green

With the spell bringing Zal along behind her, Zara led the way out into the streets. The sun had been up for some time, but Azamed's business day was just dawning. Shop doors and shutters were flung open. Market stalls and carts lined the streets. Merchandise and produce spilled from the shops and onto tables, shelves and sometimes even the pavement. The streets were awash with sellers and shoppers, all rushing about, shouting and arguing, laughing and crying. Oxen, cattle and even a few dragons and desert gryphons were led through the crowds by their careful owners. The scent of food – grain, fruit and meat – filled the air. The two biggest items for sale were new blooming flowers and beautifully woven racing carpets.

As Zal had said, the race was on everyone's mind. Flags with the race symbol fluttered everywhere. Signs in the windows of restaurants and pubs advertised good balconies to view it from. Printers worked non-stop to produce maps and score cards, and dozens of bards, minstrels and storytellers were busy singing of past races and their contestants.

Zara and Zal moved through the crowds, with Rip weaving around people's legs and barking at any dog or cat smaller than him.

"Let me go!" Zal shouted, both from rage and to be heard over the noise of the market.

"Stop making a fuss!"

"Making a fuss? Give me my legs back!"

The spell had not gone quite as smoothly as Zara had intended: it made Zal take steps that were either too big or too small, and every fifth one veered slightly to the left. Zal knocked over two baskets of pomegranates, broke an oil jar and shook the perch of a blue and yellow parrot that screeched loudly in his ear.

"It's not as if I've taken them off you," Zara said.

"You know what I mean. Reverse the spell now, and... Where are we going?"

"To prove to you that rainbow carpets are real," Zara replied. "And then to find out how to weave one. That flies."

"But rainbow carpets aren't real. They're impossible!"

"Trust me."

"Trust you? Give me back my legs!"

The rainbow carpet was the greatest legend of Azamed. The best carpets were those that mixed several colours: the more, the better. In all logic, the ultimate carpet included all seven – a rainbow carpet. It would have every advantage and, in theory, no disadvantages. But making one seemed to be impossible.

Myths said that it was possible. The legendary Blue Caliph had apparently owned one, which he'd ridden many times to defend the city from the Serpent Hordes and the Fuj Empire. He had really been Caliph Lubun the Fourth but had been called the Blue Caliph after an unfortunate accident during a tour of a paint factory. Even after the colour had finally faded, the name had stuck. But he had been three Caliphs before Caliph Rabo the First, in whose reign Azamed had discovered writing and begun properly recording its history. Any stories from before that, such as Caliph Hasa the Mad defending Azamed from invasion by a race of giant fish, were suspect. After all, how would fish have crossed the desert?

Whatever the truth of the legends, no one in living memory or recorded history had ever succeeded in weaving a seven-colour rainbow carpet. This was not for want of trying: two or three people came up with a new idea and tried it out each year. Zal had even seen a couple of attempts. The carpets had been woven with all seven colours, and their structures were sound; a seven-colour magician had come to add the magic, and then the project had failed. Seven-colour carpets would not retain magic. It flowed from the magician's hands, into the weaving, and then spilt straight out again in hopeless, muddled confusion. No carpet-weaver had found a pattern or material or combination of both that could hold in all seven colours. No magician had found a way of stopping the spillage. No rainbow carpet had ever left the ground.

There were various theories as to why this was. No one could balance all seven just right; the seven colours of magic repelled each other at such close quarters; the Celestial Stork disliked the number seven; the giant fish had placed a curse on the combination as revenge for their defeat by Caliph Hasa, and so on. The most popular theory was that carpet wool could only contain a certain amount of magic, in the same way as a sponge could only hold so much water: something else would be needed to hold it in. Various materials and alchemical coatings had been tried, but none had worked. In Azamed, the seven-colour rainbow carpet was regarded as being too close to impossible to be worth the time. The songs and stories of the Blue Caliph were still savoured by children, but only a fool would try to weave one.

"Where are we going?" Zal shouted.

"I just told you!"

"No. Where, in the city, are we going?"

"The Guild, of course! Where else?"

Zal remembered the age-old adage that the mad should be humoured and decided to keep quiet for the rest of the journey. He concentrated on trying to get back control of his legs by willpower as he followed Zara along the streets, over the bridges and up and down the public stairways that wound around Azamed's mountain.

At one landing, he looked out across the yellow desert and saw in the distance a long caravan crawling its way towards Azamed from the west. It must have come from Endsali or Caldyn or one of the other giant ports that existed where the desert became the ocean, thousands of miles away. Great ships from other continents carried manufactured items across the waves from the far west to the ports: pots and pans, tools and weapons. These were loaded onto the caravans and sent across the desert to Azamed, where they would meet other caravans coming from the rainforests to the east. These would carry raw materials: ores, timber, cloth and precious stones. In Azamed they would be exchanged and traded. The manufactured goods would go where they were required in the east and the raw materials would be carried across both the desert and the ocean to where they were needed in the factories of other continents. The Caliph of Azamed taxed every transaction, and so the city grew and flourished.

The Guild of Magicians was as old as the city. The Shadow Society – their greatest competition – was fifteen years younger. The Guild was a union of close to all the magicians in Azamed and it decided on the prices members could charge for their services and what was acceptable business practice. For example, a Guild magician could charge three gold pieces for successfully curing a camel's fear of bats, but they could only charge one and a half gold pieces if their solution was to make the camel wear a blindfold. The Guild also owned the second largest library in Azamed and ran one of the city's two schools for children gifted with magic. The other school was run by the Shadow Society.

Zal had passed the high walls around the Guild school many times, but he had never before been inside them: the grounds were for staff and pupils only. Zara led him up to the large gate and knocked.

"Who goes?" came a deep voice from the other side.

"Zara Aura, Rainbow House and … her intended husband. And dog."

"No—" Zal began.

"Shut up, Zal." The gates opened a fraction and

Zara dragged him through, Rip hopping in after them. Zal looked around and was surprised to see no one on the gates on the other side.

"Where did the gatekeeper go?"

"What gate…? Oh! There isn't one," said Zara. She reached back and tapped the wood of the gate. "It's the gates themselves."

"Welcome to the Guild, young sir," said the deep voice. "If you are lucky, you may leave alive and intact."

"Oh!" said Zal. "Well … um … thank—"

"Yes, thank you," said Zara and pulled Zal away. "Never talk with talking gates," she advised, "any more than you need to. If you start a conversation, it can take hours to get through them."

As they walked through the grounds of the Guild towards the main building, Zal looked around with great interest. They were surrounded by very beautiful gardens. There were long green lawns, each blade of grass enchanted to grow to exactly the same length. The flower-beds were brilliant jungles of miniature trees with trunks as long and thick as fingers. Giant carnivorous plants grew in the corners, all spikes and spines, and their branches darted out every few seconds to snatch insects from the air.

"Keep your distance from those," Zara advised.

There were also ornate fountains and small waterfalls where the water flowed up instead of down, and in circles, spirals and corkscrews through mid-air, glistening white and gold in the sunlight. Dozens of small birds and butterflies filled the air with soft songs and calls and the rustling beat of their wings. None ever seemed to fly higher than the wall. The scent of pomegranates drifted from a grove of trees where the fruit grew all the way up and down the trunks.

Zal was particularly fascinated by the students. Zara wasn't one to show off her magic, but what he saw here impressed him a great deal. There were students sitting in a circle three feet off the ground as they enjoyed their breaktime outside. One of the larger fountains had a wide pond, and seven students were walking – even running – on the water as they played a ball game. Another rather plump boy was standing calm and poised as he made giant, jagged crystals sprout from the ground in fantastic colours. A moment later he was running about in terror as they began sprouting from his hands.

"That's Hani," said Zara. "He's talented but a bit hasty. He'll be fine in a while. He's in my house and he's also competing in the race."

A teacher reached Hani and began removing the crystals from the sobbing boy.

"Your house?" said Zal.

"School house," Zara said. "There are eight. One for each colour, and Rainbow House for multi-colours like me."

Most of Azamed's magicians were born at the instant when the Celestial Stork beat her wings, sweeping her magic into the world. However, it helped if one or both of your parents was a magician, as Zara's mother had been. Most magicians were born with only one colour of magic within them. Those who contained more than one colour were rare, so their services were very much in demand. Some contained more colours than others, and the very rarest held seven colours like Zara. She only knew of eight others like her in Azamed but suspected Haragan might be a ninth. They were almost never out of work and Arna Aura was confident he could spend a very comfortable retirement on Zara's eventual earnings.

"Right," said Zal. "So where are we going?"

"To see Qwinton. My favourite teacher."

The Guild building was a disappointment to Zal. After the wonders that had filled the gardens, it seemed far too plain, ordinary and practical. He expected to see a miracle round every corner but instead was lucky if he saw a mop. Zara led him and Rip up to the fourth floor, which a sign identified as the teachers' rooms. The door bearing the name "Qwinton" was the third they came to.

"Before we meet him," said Zara, "you should know that he once had an accident with a Cassiak spell."

"A what?" said Zal.

"He's a bit bonkers," she said, and knocked.

There was a high-pitched scream from the other side of the door.

"Just a minute! Just a minute! Everything's fine! Fine! Perfectly fine!"

"It's Zara, Master Qwinton," Zara said. "Could we come in, please?"

"Zara? Wait a minute… We? We! There's more than one of you?"

"No," Zara said. "There's just one of me, and

my friend. Can we come in, please? I need your counsel."

"My counsel? You need my counsel? Well, that changes everything!" The door flew open, revealing Qwinton. He was a short man with a ruffled beard and rumpled clothes, and his thick glasses had become askew on his nose from all his bustling about. "Come in, come in, my dear. And who are your friends here?"

"This is Zal Thesa …"

"A pleasure! A pleasure, my dear boy."

"Hello." They shook hands.

"… and his dog, Rip."

"His dog? AAAAAAAAARGH!" Qwinton jumped back into the very untidy room and fell backwards over a chair, landing with a crash. Then he looked again at the puzzled Rip. "Oh, wait! It's a dog. That's all. Just a dog. Please, come in. Come in."

"Thank you," said Zara with a big, reassuring smile. She pulled Zal into the room and kicked the door shut behind them.

"Sit down," said Qwinton. "Take a seat. Take the chairs, the bed, tables, floor, walls, ceiling. It makes no difference where."

"Thank you very much," said Zal. He sat down on the edge of the bed. Zara sat beside him and Rip leapt up onto his lap.

"Ah! A jumping dog," Qwinton nodded, his beard trembling. "That's good. Very good. A sign of health and activity."

"I make sure he takes plenty of exercise, sir," said Zal. He had always been taught to be polite to magicians. He felt this to be of double importance in the Guild school, where it was rumoured that if you talked in lessons you could be punished by being turned into a beetle for your entire lunch break.

"Splendid! Splendid!" said Qwinton.

"Thank you for seeing us, sir," said Zara. She was about to say more, but Qwinton launched off again.

"Ah, yes! So many of my colleagues would have turned you away like an undercooked fish in a restaurant. But then, they're not as addled as I am. And I should know, I cast the spell that did it. None of the others has come close."

"Really?" said Zal, causing Zara to scowl at him.

"Yes! I cast the spell that addled me. Well, hitting

my head on that low branch while flying my carpet backwards might have done something. It might even have made me get the spell wrong. But it *was* the spell. All my own work!"

"Yes, Master," said Zara. "But I was hoping you could tell us something about rainbow carpets."

"Rainbow carpets? Rainbow carpets... Aha! This is because the race is drawing near, isn't it?"

"Yes, sir. I'm afraid so," said Zara.

"No need to apologize, my dear," said Qwinton. He bounced to his feet, rubbing his hands together. "I can do a lot better than tell you about it. I can, and I'm going to, show you my greatest, most secret, most precious treasure, which I keep so safe and so secret that it is almost sanctified!"

He stopped and looked around.

"Now then, where did I put it?"

Qwinton began rummaging in his wardrobe, throwing clothes and books over his shoulder. Six white doves fluttered out and perched around the room, venting soft coos.

Zara leant close to Zal and whispered, "He's shown it to me twice before. He has a very short memory."

"Found it!" Qwinton cried. He turned round, holding a small wooden chest with a large bronze lock. "Now, where did I put the key?"

"It seems to be in the lock," said Zal, pointing at the chest.

"Oh, of course!" said Qwinton. "I put it in the last place a thief would think of looking for it. But you two are not thieves, so go ahead."

Zara took the chest and placed it on the table. She turned the key and opened the lid. Zal leant over her shoulder, and Rip placed his front paws on the table top for a better view. Zara lifted a small roll of material out of the box and unrolled it across the table surface.

Zal gasped as it unfurled.

It had been torn from the end of a carpet. A rainbow carpet. All seven colours of the rainbow were present in it, stretching from its tasselled edge to its ragged one. It was only a fragment of a whole carpet, but it shimmered with the unmistakable gleam of magic. It had been enchanted, the magic had been retained and Zal's weaving knowledge told him without a single doubt that the carpet had flown.

"It's beautiful," he said. It was. It was old and the

colours had faded, as if they were layered in dust, but it still shone beneath. A pattern of amazing complexity had been woven into it, and Zal found himself longing to repeat it. Zara smiled at his reaction, and touched the carpet with her hand. It trembled. A wave ran down from one end to the other, and then the fragment floated up from the table top and hovered for a long moment before sinking back down.

"Seeing it do that makes me wish I had been a weaver," said Qwinton.

"It's real," said Zal. "They *are* real!"

"Told you so," said Zara. "Thank you for showing it to us, Master Qwinton."

Rip sniffed the fragment and gave an approving yip.

"It's real," said Zal again.

"Indeed it is," said Qwinton. "You don't think I'd waste my precious time protecting a worthless fake, do you?"

"Well ... now that we've settled that part of the argument," said Zara, turning to Zal, "do you think you can weave one?"

"I ... um..."

Zal picked up the fragment with very careful hands. He ran his fingertips across the weaving, feeling exactly where each thread began and ended. It was a strange and intricate work. The colours were not just flat: each was made of hundreds of tones of that colour, light and dark, woven together. The extra power that must give to the carpet made Zal's mind ache. Each stitch seemed to be perfect.

"Well?" said Zara.

"Whoever wove this," said Zal, "must have used a needle that was thinner than a strand of spider's web."

"There are many good blacksmiths in the city…"

"There's something else," Zal said, tracing the fragment from end to end again. "I don't know what it is, but I don't think it's magic."

"Let me try." Zara reached and touched the fragment with her fingertips. "Where is it?"

"It's everywhere."

Qwinton was busy cooing to one of the doves and feeding it crumbs from a cheese biscuit.

"I don't feel anything," said Zara.

"It's there," Zal said. "And I've got a feeling that that is what makes – what made – it fly. The missing ingredient. The thing that holds the magic in."

Almost without him realizing it, Zal's weaving knowledge came into play. His voice became businesslike.

"I can get wool that's thin enough, and there must be this many tones of each colour in the city. And you're right: the blacksmith who forged my sword should be able to make the needles. But this ... mystery ingredient. I don't know what it is or where to get it."

"Ah, mysteries," said Qwinton. "They fill our hours with boundless entertainment. Who doesn't enjoy a good word game? Fun, fun, fun, fun, fun. But at the same time they irritate, infuriate and, on occasion, asphyxiate us. A good mystery is a paradox. And a paradox is often a good mystery."

"Yes, but how do we solve this one in" – Zara looked out of the window at the sun. It was now halfway across the sky. Noon – "half a day and a night?"

"We can't," said Zal. He patted Rip and felt sadness, and still some amazement at the fragment of carpet.

"Now, now!" said Qwinton. He snatched up a

ruler and rapped Zal across the head with it. "That's defeatism. I'll have none of that here. Defeatism has no place outside a maths exam. That fragment alone is proof that anything is possible."

"But even if we find it, the race is tomorrow morning," Zal said. "It took me three weeks to weave the six-colour carpet. I'll never be able to do a full-sized seven-colour one in less than a day and a night!"

"Don't worry," said Zara, "I have that covered."

"How?"

"Oh, you don't need to know yet. I'll surprise you when we get there. You'll like it."

"Fine," said Zal. "But even if you can do it, which I doubt, we still don't know where to get the mystery ingredient from."

"Then we'll find out," said Zara, rubbing her hands together. "Master Qwinton, where did you get the fragment from?"

"The fragment? Oh – of course, the fragment. It is remarkable, isn't it! And there's a strange story behind how it came into my possession. I found it half buried on the shore of the Small Oasis. What stranger place could there be to find a fragment of carpet? I spent weeks digging around there, first with a spade, then with magic so I could be more thorough, and then with a magic spade, but I never found another strand of it. It's a mystery."

"You can say that again," said Zal.

"It's a mystery," said Qwinton. "I'm old and tired now and addled by my own hand, but if I wanted to solve it, I would start at the Caliph's library. All the secrets and mysteries of Azamed are stored within its walls, you know, and I once heard a rumour that he has some documents on rainbow carpets, written by Rabo the First himself."

"Excellent," said Zara. "That's perfect. That's where we'll start. Thank you, Master Qwinton. Come on, Zal!"

Zara grabbed Zal's wrist again and pulled him from the room.

"Good luck!" Qwinton said as he closed the door.

"Wha…? Wait!" said Zal. "The Caliph's library?"

Twenty minutes later they had climbed up the steep streets to the Caliph's palace and were approaching the public entrance.

"You're crazy," said Zal. "We can't sneak into the

Caliph's private library and start reading his scrolls. How's he likely to react if he catches us? He'll have us thrown in the dungeons!"

"I'd imagine so," said Zara, not at all concerned at the prospect. "If that happens, I'll use magic to open the locks, then we'll sneak back to the library and finish what we started."

"What kind of mad…?" Zal began.

"What kind of mad person would search a library for thieves twice in one day?" Zara finished for him. "Well done: you're catching on." She jogged up the steps to the palace and Zal and Rip had to run to keep up.

"I am not 'catching on'," called Zal. "I'm trying to talk some sense into you. This is a stupid idea. We need to try something else."

"Really? Then why are you following me?" Zara smiled.

"Because you've got this stupid spell on my legs, that's why!"

"Zal, come here," said Zara.

Zal did not move. He was startled when he realized he hadn't.

"It wore off while we were with Qwinton," said

Zara. "You've been following me of your own accord ever since. You can go back now if you want to …"

Zal still did not move.

"… but that would mean losing the chance to be the first weaver in centuries to produce a rainbow carpet. And now you know they're real…"

Zal hesitated, thinking carefully. To turn back now was the sane option. But Zara was right about the carpet. And could he really, in all good con-science – even though she was so annoying – let her go and get herself arrested? He walked up the steps, trying hard to ignore her smirk.

The Caliph's palace was built on top of two giant stone bridges that spanned the volcano's crater and met in an X shape. It had taken one hundred archi-tects two hundred years to build, but they had done a very good job. Zal and Zara were entering from the eastern side, which led into the Mosaic Gardens. Inside the high, round walls were flower-beds, enchanted to be in bloom all year round, and huge, detailed mosaics made of tiny slivers of terracotta, marble and glass that depicted carpets and the Great Race.

This was the only area of the palace open to the

public, and there weren't many people around: a few families who'd brought children to play; elderly people who sat on the benches and argued; an artist painting a picture of a very beautiful flower that he alone could see. A few white storks, kept in honour of the Celestial Stork, were in the fountains eating breadcrumbs thrown by the children.

There were steps at the far end that led into the palace, and Zara headed towards these. Zal looked with great admiration at the guardsman who stood at the top of them, leaning on his spear and chewing a blade of grass. This was where he would one day stand – if you could still become a guardsman after assisting your insane fiancée in trespass and burglary. Zal gulped. His future and his dreams were teetering on a cliff edge, and Zara might just be about to kick them over.

"Let me do the talking," Zara whispered and marched up the steps.

The guardsman straightened and opened his mouth to inform them that they could go no further.

"Good morning," Zara said. "Has my master come through here?"

"Your master?" asked the guardsman, puzzled.

"Yes, my master."

"I'm not sure," said the guardsman.

"Has he come through here, or not?" Zara said.

"I don't know."

"Well, have you seen him, or not?"

"I'm not sure!"

"You're not sure if you have or have not seen my master come through here, or not?"

"Not... I mean, no. I don't know who your master is!" The guardsman was becoming rather agitated. He leant back away from Zara and gripped his spear.

"Well, how about his associates?" Zara said.

"No..."

"His colleagues?"

"No."

"His friends?"

"No!"

"His enemies?"

Zara ticked them off on her fingers as she recited them. The list continued through "her master's" confidantes, spies, assassins, speechwriters, joke-writers, elder siblings, parents, children, grandchildren, cousins, nephews, wife and any or all of his mistresses. The poor guardsman became more and more distressed at the huge number of people who seemed to have slipped into the palace under his nose. Rip dozed off on the top step. Zal watched Zara's performance with astonishment and decided he sympathized with Arna Aura's desire to marry off his daughter as soon as possible.

"His banker?"

"Stop!" The guard's shout made everybody in the garden look up. "Who is your master? Tell me that, and I can answer your first question."

"You can?" said Zara. She turned to Zal. "What was my first question? It's slipped my mind."

Zal panicked. He couldn't remember either.

"Whether or not your master has come through here," said the guardsman.

"Oh, yes. That was it," said Zara. "Has he?"

"If you'll tell me who he is, I can tell you!"

"Oh, of course! Forgive me."

The guard's expression suggested that would not be happening fast.

"I am Zara Aura of the Guild of Magicians. My master is the magician Ho-Og Wa-Ash, also of the Guild. The Caliph summoned him here today to

84

use magic to wash all the parrots in the palace menagerie without injuring any of the parrots, allowing any parrot to notice it is being washed, spilling any water, dropping the soap, or washing any other animal by accident. This has turned out to be a far more complicated task than my master imagined. He's been sending me back and forth all morning to fetch all the people I've mentioned, to see if any of them can help. This is the latest, his personal carpet-weaver and fencing partner, Zal Thesa."

"Hello," said Zal.

"I see," the guardsman said to Zara.

"I'm so glad," said Zara. "Now, if you haven't seen him or any of the others, they must have all gone straight to the menagerie. We'll go down there, Zal, and try not to get lost. Those parrots won't wash themselves!"

"Go to the main hall and take the blue door to the west wing," said the guard, pointing down the corridor and standing aside so Zara and Zal could pass through.

"Thanks so much!" Zara called back.

"Hold on a second!"

They stopped and turned their heads. Zal could hear the dungeon door creaking open.

"What's a carpet-weaver needed for?"

"Oh, my master thought it would help if the carpets had pictures of parrots on them," said Zara. "There aren't any in the palace that do. So he's here to weave them."

"But what do you need carpets for in a menagerie? They'll get covered in…"

"You expect the parrots to be washed while standing on a cold, stone floor?" Zara filled her voice with shock and outrage.

"But I thought the parrots mustn't realize they're being washed!"

"It's the principle!" said Zara. "Come on, Zal. We're losing time."

They hurried round the corner and out of sight before the guard could say anything else.

"I'm not sure which is more unbelievable," said Zal. "That you tried that, or that it worked."

"Where there's a will, there's a way," said Zara smugly.

"Fine, but when I get into the Guard, I'm warning everyone about that trick. That is, if I can even get my application looked at after this…"

"Stop worrying. You've got carpets to fall back on."

"I hate carpet-weaving."

"But you're very good at it."

"That doesn't mean I like it."

"It's still the reason your father hasn't given up on you."

They hurried on, exploring the palace. It was a fantastic building. Travellers who came across the desert said that when you climbed the last dune and could see all of Azamed for the first time, the palace shone brighter than any other building. It was just as spectacular inside. Everywhere was designed to be both functional and attractive. The corridors were wide with smooth tiled floors and high, arching ceilings. At every corner, imps carved from black marble and cherubs carved from white leered and laughed down at them from the walls. The walls were all painted white or a soft green, but the skirting boards were decorated with fantastic miniature paintings and murals, like a long, tiny tapestry. The Celestial Stork, the Cosmos Vulture and a pantheon of monsters, heroes, demons and angels, together with thousands of magic carpets, flowed along the base of the walls. Though they were small, they had been painted with all the detail and determination that had gone into the Mosaic Gardens.

Zal and Zara barely noticed. Zara was set on finding the library and Zal was still thinking about her last words. Had Augur ever considered giving up on him? He wouldn't be surprised. Zal had argued for hours, thrown temper tantrums and kicked furniture over to try and get out of carpet-weaving, but his father had always slowly and patiently persuaded him to do it. Now he thought about it, if Augur had ever really wanted to force him to weave, he could simply have confiscated Zal's sword, dismissed his fencing teacher and forbade him from entering tournaments. But instead he'd used calm persistence to get Zal to the loom – and had also paid for his fencing classes, bought him a new sword whenever he needed one, and cheered Zal from the front row at every tournament.

"Oh, and if anyone stops us, stick with 'We're here to wash parrots,' OK?" said Zara, breaking into his thoughts.

"Sorry, what?"

"Oh, never mind. It doesn't matter. We're here now."

She stopped him before a tall, wooden door which had on it a bronze plaque that read, LIBRARY. Zara turned the handle but it took both of them to push open the heavy door. They peered round it before entering, but there was no movement and no sound from among the bookshelves. The trio slipped inside.

The sheer size of the library inspired reverence. The ceiling was so high, it looked no larger than a handkerchief. The shelves stretched all the way up to it, running right round the walls of the hall. Groups of shelves were divided up into small octagons, each packed with numerous tight rolls of parchment. It was like standing inside a gigantic wood and paper honeycomb. There were thousands of scrolls. Some were thicker or thinner than their companions. Some had writing on both sides and some did not. Some stuck out past the edge of the shelves, and some were tucked so far back that they were almost invisible. The door and several tall narrow windows that let in shafts of light were the only breaks in the pattern. The silence was heavy, and their breathing seemed as loud as an orchestra. The dry, cool smell of paper and parchment was in the air. Zal and Zara both jumped and spun round as the door banged shut behind them.

"Here to wash parrots," Zal agreed as he breathed out. He offered a quick prayer to the Celestial Stork that they would not be caught.

"Just keep quiet and we'll be fine," said Zara. "All the secrets and mysteries of Azamed? I can believe that."

"Yes," said Zal. "But where do we start looking?" They both stood, staring up at the towering bookshelves. Rip huddled close to Zal's ankles and whimpered. Rooms were not meant to be this big. Only the outside was.

Zara, for the first time that day, found herself without an answer. Zal was right. There were no labels on the shelves, no catalogues to hand. Why would there be? This was for the Caliph and his family alone. Finding the secret of the rainbow carpet could take years. And how to narrow that down...

"I don't have a clue," she said.

They walked to the shelves closest to the door and began pulling out random scrolls and reading the titles printed on the brown wax seals that kept them closed.

In the first octagon, Zal found *The Saga of Renguard, The Plant Life of the Cold Jungle, Northern Azamed By Night, The Dynamics of a Waterfall* and *Daniel the Donkey.*

"There's no order to them," he said. "I've got mythology, science, tourism and a children's story all from the same shelf."

"I know," said Zara. She held up the scrolls in her hand. "I've got philosophy, agriculture, magic and soup cooking. How does the Caliph ever find anything?"

"How are *we* ever going to find anything?" Zal said. He gazed up at the shelves again and then asked, "Can you do something with magic?"

Before Zara could reply, Rip gave a sudden yap, catching their attention. He had wandered off to the far side of the room and was sniffing at the legs of a table. It had an old, fading scent spiralled around it that would probably get swept away the next time the room was dusted. But Rip recognized it. He'd smelt it not long ago in Qwinton's room when Zara opened the chest.

"What is it, boy?" Zal asked as he and Zara walked over. They saw that the table was actually a display case with a glass lid, and that inside...

"Holy Stork!" said Zal. "It's another fragment!"

It was. Another torn section of rainbow carpet. It was older, more frayed and ragged than Qwinton's treasure, but it had flown. The magic still glistened on the threads like tiny stars.

"Amazing," said Zara. "Qwinton has to know about this one as well. He must just have forgotten why he was telling us to look in the library."

"It's unbelievable," said Zal. "What's this here?"

He had stepped to the side and was examining the other part of the case. A large sheet of yellowed parchment, as dry and fragile as a fallen autumn leaf, was stretched out in it. Its surface was covered in writing in faded blue ink. The script and characters were alien to Zal. He had seen nothing like them before. But he *had* seen...

"Aha!" Zara pointed to the small symbol printed in the top corner. "The seal of Caliph Rabo the First himself! This is it. Well done, Rip!"

Zal was absorbed in the small drawings on the parchment. Blood, fire, flesh, plants, the sun, the sky, water … the physical incarnations of the seven colours, all sketched in ink at the parchment's edges. There was also a drawing of a strange spider and some sort of cliff edge, a small section where a large crack appeared in the rock wall.

"Hey," said Zara. She pointed at the last sketch. "I know that!"

"You know it?"

"I recognize it," Zara said, gazing at the drawing.

"How could you recognize it? This scroll is a thousand years old!"

"Trust me," said Zara. "I know where that is, and it's where we need to go. I'll explain on the way. Come on."

Zal was about to follow, when something else caught his eye. A gleam from the other side of the room.

"Hold on," he said. "What's that?"

He led the way over to another table, which had a chair before it. An ink pot, a jar of quills and several rolls of blank parchment were arranged on it in a careless way.

"It must be the Caliph's writing desk," said Zara.

"Look," said Zal.

He moved one of the scrolls aside. Beneath it, in a small jewellery box, was the largest, most beautiful diamond ring either of them had ever seen. The stone was blue-white and the sunlight from the windows blazed on its corners and edges like tiny stars. A cooling light of its own seemed to glow from within it. It was mounted on a slim gold ring carved with a pattern of interwoven leaves.

"That's beautiful," said Zara. "Holy Stork! I'm so tempted to try it on."

"I'm tempted to do something else," said Zal.

"What?"

"Take it," said Zal. He gazed at the ring, longing in his eyes. "Be honest. Our chances of finding this rainbow carpet secret are small. This is worth a lot more than ten thousand gold pieces."

He looked at Zara.

"It would solve all our problems in one go."

There was a long pause. They both looked at the ring.

"You've got a point," said Zara. "It's sure to be a lot easier than whatever lies ahead."

"We could rebuild and restock the shop in a few days," Zal said.

The ring sat there and whispered to them in a soft, tempting tone.

Zal opened his hand. It was inches away. It would be so simple just to reach out...

"The shop could be better than it was before," said Zara. "Dad and I could get our kitchen decorated at last..."

"There would be more than enough to share," said Zal. His hand and wrist throbbed. The jewel stopped its whispering and began to sing – the most beautiful, seductive tune Zal had ever heard. Its lyrics were promises of possibility.

"But I don't know," said Zara, biting her lip. Her hands were also aching. It was tempting.

"It's probably a present for one of his daughters, isn't it?" Zal said. "And if I take it..."

"There'd be hell to pay if we were caught," said Zara. "We'd be ruined. Again. But I can use magic to cover up everything that proves we were in here. We could re-carve it before we sell it. I think we *could* get away with it."

"But we still wouldn't be in the race," said Zal.

"And we'd be no better than the Shadow Society."

Zal shook himself and relaxed his arm. "No. I can't do it."

"You're right. Me neither."

"It was a stupid idea."

"Yes."

They stood gazing at the jewel for another minute.

"Let's go and find that place on the map."

"Yes."

They turned and walked purposefully away from the seductive stone and closed the library door behind them.

"It was an easy way out," said Zal.

"Yes," agreed Zara. "We wouldn't have got anything from it."

"Let's walk faster."

"Excellent idea."

They resisted the temptation to turn back and travelled, without discovery, through the palace, back the way they had come. The jewel's song faded away with the sound of their footsteps in the empty halls.

Blue

They passed the same guard on their way out.

"Oh," he said. "Hello. Again."

"Hello," said Zara. "Sorry we can't stop."

"Yes," said Zal, keen to join in. "The master now needs his butler, his blackmailer and his singlestick-maker. And I need some more tools."

"Please wish them luck," said the guard, who was pondering early retirement.

They left the gardens and Zara led the way round the crater's rim. This was a circle of space between the city and the palace. The ground slope, ragged and tufted with grass, was far too steep for houses to be built on. It was a wasteland that nobody did anything with, save for the children who enjoyed it as a playground. Zal and Zara scrambled along the slope like crabs, using their hands as well as their feet. Zal stuck close behind Zara, who seemed to know exactly where they were going. She talked as they hurried along.

"About two years ago," she said, "some friends and I got into trouble at school."

"What for?"

"We were all sick and tired of the headmaster's cat," Zara replied, vaulting over a boulder. "A huge, horrible black thing. It always took the best chairs in the common room and scratched anyone who tried to share. Hani's still got the scars. So a few of us got together, and we decided to even the score."

"How?" Zal followed her over the boulder and Rip ran round it.

"Well, when the cat wasn't scratching or biting, it was catching mice. That was the one thing it was good for. So we used that against it."

"How?"

"We caught a mouse alive and enchanted it so it could bite through steel."

"Wow!" said Zal.

"The showdown was brilliant." Zara smiled at the memory.

"It must have been, by the Stork! I'd have loved to have seen it," said Zal.

"I did think about inviting you," Zara said, "but it was the week after the Under 10s fencing contest, when we weren't talking to each other. Anyway, the head didn't think it was as funny as we did. We hadn't learned enough magic to cover our tracks – they found out who we all were in five minutes. The punishment was to run fifty laps round here, casting as many basic spells as we could without stopping. Horrible, difficult and exhausting."

Zal slipped and sent a small avalanche of pebbles and stones rumbling down the slope. He pulled himself up again.

"Did you manage it?"

"It almost killed us, but yes," Zara said, looking around her. "And on the way round, we passed ... this!"

And there it was. A cleft in the lip of the volcano, just as it had been drawn on the parchment.

"Brilliant!" said Zal. "But what's special about it?"

"Let's find out."

Rip got there first and pushed his nose through the bottom of the crack. He sniffed and yipped to say it was safe. Zal and Zara, of course, did not understand him and peered in with great caution.

"Hmmm," they said together.

The crack was a narrow – possibly camouflaged – opening to three large stone steps that began to lead down into the volcano. The edge of the bottom step was jagged and crumbled. There had once been more steps, but they had collapsed long ago. Zara stepped through the crack and touched the top step with a careful foot. It didn't shift or shudder.

"It feels OK."

Zal stepped through beside her, then twisted to pick up Rip and lift him through. The three of them peeped over the bottom step. There was nothing but darkness to be seen below.

"There was a way down," Zal said. "To something."

"The secret of the carpet fragments?" Zara wondered.

"Well, maybe. But something else as well. A staircase into the crater is a lot to build. I wonder what it was."

"You'll soon find out," said a voice behind them.

Zal and Zara spun round so fast that they almost knocked each other off the edge. Rip barked in surprise.

"Haragan!" Zara yelled.

It was indeed him, wrapped in brown as always and seated on his carpet, which floated above the crack. He radiated triumph and smugness.

"The very same," he said. "And I continue to be amazed by your stupidity."

"Come down here and say that!" Zal started to draw his scimitar, then realized there was so little arm space on the steps that he was liable to cut himself.

"Try following two people around all morning with neither of them spotting you, and you'll reconsider."

"I know it was you last night," Zara breathed, bubbling with fury. Her fists were clenched and even Rip could feel her magic building.

"Of course it was," said Haragan. "But do you really think I consider you such easy meat that I'd wreck your carpet and all your materials and then say job done? We know each other better than that."

Zal had managed to draw his scimitar and now

faced the problem of how to swing it without hurting Zara. He stalled for time.

"What do you want?"

"To ensure my victory in the race before it has begun," Haragan said.

"I'm going to cut you out of the air, Haragon!" said Zal.

"Hara*gan*," said Haragan. "And you're not. But thank you for setting out on this quest. By following you, I've seen all the threats to my victory that still remain. I'm now off to neutralize them. You two, however, have some falling to do."

Zara shot up her hand and cast magic, but Haragan was ready. He deflected it with his right hand and used his left to shoot a separate bolt, aimed not at Zara but at the join between the steps and the volcano wall. The rock disintegrated in an explosion of dust. The steps broke free and plummeted downwards like a hailstone. Zal didn't hear Zara's scream. Filled with rage, he had launched himself forward, sword raised. He was ready to leap up to the level of Haragan's carpet, but the ground vanished from under him. He fell short but succeeded in slashing a ten-inch cut into the carpet, causing it to lurch in the air. His other hand reached for Haragan's neck. Haragan flinched backwards and Zal grabbed hold of his medallion. The chain went taut, broke, and then Zal was falling, feet first, into the darkness.

Haragan scrambled backwards on his carpet and toppled off the back edge onto the crater ledge. Magic flying at his face was one thing. He was used to that. But a long, sharp scimitar blade was quite another. Haragan dropped to the ground, panting and trembling. The speed and accuracy with which the sword had moved ... the gleam in Thesa's eye... He had thought for an instant that he was going to be sliced in half. Haragan gripped a nearby rock to stop his hands from shaking. He tried to slow his breathing.

He quickly offered a prayer of thanks to the Cosmos Vulture – something, he was ashamed to admit, he didn't do as often as he should. He had been terrified ... but ... it was over.

It was over at last.

Haragan breathed out and found himself remembering how it had begun.

Five years ago. A hot summer afternoon. There

were two kinds of afternoon in summer: heavy ones, where the heat weighed down your limbs and made every movement difficult; and electric ones, where you could taste the charge and the sparkle of lightning in the air. The afternoon of the Under 10s magic contest had been an electric one for him and a heavy one for everyone else.

The contest was being held on the flat grey flagstones of the eastern market square, a place filled with bright awnings over stalls of fruit and vegetables, and plenty of Azamed's beautiful flowers. They, at least, with their dazzling colours, seemed to be cheering him on. If his life had been different, Haragan mused, a career as a florist – no, a gardener – would have suited him down to the ground.

He was pulled away from his happy daydream by his opponent at the other end of the spell-casting diamond. The boy, a student from the Magician's Guild who was plump and called Hani-something, flung a nervous, clumsy spell in his direction. Haragan did not even glance to see what the spell was. He batted it aside with one hand and fired back an Endless River spell with the other. It hit the other boy square in the face and he fell backwards with a moaning howl as he burst into tears. One of the Guild teachers ran forward to help him up and then led the sobbing boy over to a side bench to join three over contestants who were weeping with the same fury. Endless River spells, which made it impossible to stop crying for three hours, were Haragan's trademark.

The young Haragan was on a roll. The contest had been running for an hour, and he was one match away from victory. He'd been the first Shadow candidate to step forward. No one had yet needed to replace him, as he'd beaten every other contestant hands down. He'd avoided stun spells, blocked bone-stealing spells and thwarted three attempts to turn him into a gibbon. He'd responded with Endless River spells and blinding Sunbeam spells and had even turned one wealthy, home-schooled girl into an iguana. All those who'd faced him were now slumped, exhausted and beaten, in among the spectators, who clapped with tired politeness each time he won.

The clapping filled him with grim satisfaction. Haragan loved magical contests. It was the only life he had outside the Society. He had no family save for his fellow students and teachers and no home besides his tiny room at the headquarters. He had been abandoned as a baby and snatched up by the Shadow Society before any of Azamed's hospitals could find him and offer him up for adoption. The Society magicians had sensed his ability to cast all seven colours of magic and saw nothing in him but potential. He had not been invited into the order, as most recruits were; he had been given no choice at all.

Haragan had never known anything but schooling and training. He had never owned or worn any clothes save for the brown uniform and mask. But he still felt the full brunt of the hatred many Azamedians held for Shadows. He'd been tripped up, shouldered and hissed at in the streets enough times. The Azamedians made their feelings known to the young Shadows because they would not dare do it to the elders. The contests were when Haragan took his own back. He was the reigning champion. He beat every contestant that came at him and he made it look easy.

As he stood, relaxed, at his end of the arena, waiting for the next and final contestant to walk forward, he wished it *was* easy. In fact it was very hard. The victories he won required years: years of practice contests with other Shadows; months of practising spells on wooden targets to cast them as fast as possible; weeks spent in the Society's library, memorizing an endless list of spells, enchantments and magical combat techniques.

He didn't do it alone, of course. Oh no, there were always others studying beside him. And there were the training masters, who appeared at odd moments to test him with questions or attack him suddenly as he walked down a corridor. They would nod when he succeeded and punish him when he failed. A mistaken answer: the next day would be spent drilling the correct one into his head. A spell getting through his defences: a day of being pummelled with it until he could stop it without thinking.

It was a brilliant and successful teaching method. The trophies Haragan had carried home showed that. But it was hard, involving early rising and very late nights. Haragan always seemed to collapse onto his bed pallet exhausted, drained of magic and with reddened fingers from writing with his quill. It was hard and never-ending. It was no way to live life, but it was the only life Haragan knew. And also the contests. They made it worth it.

"Zara Aura!"

The shout came from a judge who was also announcer and master of ceremonies. Haragan turned his attention to the blonde, angry-looking girl who stalked towards the painted diamond. (Each contestant stood on one of the two furthest points, and cast their magic only within the diamond.) She met his eyes, and the venom in her gaze startled Haragan for a moment, but he soon composed himself. An angry magician was never a good fighter. They did not concentrate; they made mistakes.

The other Shadow contestants, who had cheered with real enthusiasm when Haragan triumphed, did some sniggering as Zara Aura took her place on the diamond. These became soft jeers as she assumed a magical fighting stance and locked her attention on Haragan. Haragan relaxed. Fighting stances were double-edged. She could defend his magic better, but it would slow her down when she cast her own. But that said, Haragan noticed with interest, she

was watching his hands. Before any contest, the two opponents looked at each other – it was inevitable. Most watched their opponent's eyes, trying to spot some glint or flicker that told of a move about to be made. But it was far more sensible to watch the hands, which did the moving. She was not an amateur. The girl did know a thing or two.

The announcer judge swung a hammer and the immense bronze gong boomed. Haragan and the girl began in the same instant. Two purple spirals erupted from her palms and twirled through the air towards him. Haragan batted each aside with a separate hand and heard impressed murmuring from the judges. He sent a stun spell at her. She blocked it and then surprised him by casting another straight back. The fighting stance was not slowing her down. She cast her spells fast, one after the other like beats on a drum. Haragan matched her rhythm, blocking and counter-attacking with ease. She was very good.

Haragan sent a series of glowing, shrieking spell-worms from his right hand, to distract her while he called a Tremor spell into being with his left. This was his secret weapon, which he'd used to win fights against dozens of challenging opponents. It wasn't combat magic, so no one expected it, and Haragan knew how to make it silent and invisible. All it did was shift the ground under his opponent's feet. It startled them, distracted them – put them off balance and broke their concentration. And his next spell always broke through. Haragan had dreamt up the technique himself and told no one about it. It was simple and elegant and he was very proud of it. Who wouldn't be, for all the victories it had won him?

With an almost lazy left hand, Haragan cast the spell. He was dumbstruck to watch the girl jump two feet in the air, straight above it. He saw the gleam of triumph in her eye and heard the astonished gasp from the audience. Magic contests happened on two firm feet.

He understood in an instant. *She* had guessed. She must have been waiting her turn in the audience and watching when he used it on one of the five previous contestants. This wasn't good. She'd found a weakness. She could…

The girl cast a spell while still in the air. The Cymbal spell struck Haragan's forehead like a straight punch and knocked him flat, with the sound of an orchestra ringing in his head. He'd fallen out of the diamond. She had won. His Shadow teammates gasped. And then the audience, and other contestants, and even the announcer, cheered so loudly that Haragan thought the sky would fall in. The flagstones shook and the awnings rippled from the clapping and stamping of feet.

Dari and someone else helped Haragan to his feet just in time to watch the girl being congratulated for "such a brilliant distraction technique". And then her fat father had come surging out of the audience to embrace her and swing her round. But she had looked back at him before she was surrounded by the jubilant spectators. A fierce, triumphant smile. Up until that moment, Haragan had been dazed, dizzy and confused, not quite sure what had happened. But with that look, that smile, the one he himself had given to so many losers, he knew that she had won.

The rest of the competition had been torture. He had been forced to sit on the sidelines and watch as she went through his teammates like a camel through a cactus patch. Once the orchestra had finished playing, he had to listen too: to their moans, groans and cries of pain as – for the first time in living memory – the Shadow Society lost.

The defeat had almost crushed him. His teammates were all stunned. They had walked back to base in silence. But news of Zara Aura had spread. Passers-by smirked and pointed and stallholders laughed. Haragan could not believe it. For all his hard work and effort, he had lost. He had achieved nothing. The Shadow Society knew it too. None of his teammates would have talked unless asked straight out, but somehow the news had got back to the secret headquarters ahead of them. The whole team would be punished and disciplined, but Haragan was supposed to be the team leader; he knew the severest treatment would come to him.

The Leader was waiting to greet them when they got back. Haragan had never seen the man before but knew at first glance who he was. The Leader had not spoken, he had just taken Haragan by the shoulder and led him through the corridors and tunnels to the place where failure was punished. The Dark Room.

Thrust through the door, which faded once it was closed behind him, Haragan could not tell if the room was a cupboard or a gigantic hall. The darkness was total. He took a few steps forward, arms stretched out in front. Then a tremendous, leering face screamed into existence before him. Haragan leapt back in terror, recognizing it from a nightmare he'd had at the age of three. He landed in a pile of writhing snakes, cold and slick with acid. Jumping up, another monster charged him, sending him running through the darkness, straight into the clawed embrace of a third.

Haragan was told later that he'd spent a day in the room. A day was a long time. Monsters and demons had leered, roared and torn him apart several times. When he ran out of nightmares, real memories took their place. His training masters beat him with a fury they never had in real life. Every bully he had ever known stood over him with triumph in their eyes. His friends laughed, and then turned away from him. A man and a woman he didn't recognize, but knew to be his parents, appeared. Their lips twisted with revulsion as they pushed him away from them. The Cosmos Vulture screeched and tried to bite him as he stood before it. And last of all was Zara Aura. The room, or whatever mysterious power controlled it, re-enacted her defeat of him to perfection. It added extra humiliations too. She laughed as she stood over him. She kicked dust into his face. All the spectators were there as well, and in the room, Haragan realized how many of them he recognized from coming to watch his other matches.

He had finally been released, to stagger out, wide-eyed and sticky with sweat, to collapse on the floor at the Leader's feet. His friends were there too, and this time they waited for him to pick himself up.

And that was where it had begun. The feud between Haragan of the Shadows and Zara Aura. For the next five years they had both been in every magical contest they were eligible for. They both swept away all other contenders to face each other in the final round. And then anything could happen. Either of them could win or lose, depending on whoever had had the better idea for a new secret technique, but it was always a very close-run victory. Haragan would sit up by candlelight for nights beforehand, running through his plans and strategies. He would meditate beneath waterfalls. He would practise every technique, every movement, every heartbeat, to perfection. And still Zara Aura had a damn good chance against him.

He had never been sent back into the Dark Room. No one was a second time. The Society knew of its power to destroy men's minds. But each lost match down the years had been punished. More and more training and tests. Latrine duty. A full cleaning roster. The most monotonous missions available were sent straight to Haragan. No matter how hard he worked beforehand, it was never taken into consideration. Losing was failure, and failure was punished. After Zara Aura's third victory over him, Haragan found himself near to tears over how unfair it was.

But that did not matter now.

Haragan let go of the rock and stood up, his legs still wavering. He pulled his carpet down from its hovering height and sat on it.

It did not matter any more. The past did not matter. Because, long moments ago, he had won the final victory. He had beaten Zara Aura for good. Never again would she bounce back to bite him. The last laugh was his, and Haragan leapt up from his carpet to laugh out loud and dance around the crater's lip.

He had done it. He had won.

All that was left to do was to win the race.

Haragan jumped onto his carpet and began to fly. The front edge, where Thesa's sword had gone through, flapped back, and the carpet came to a stop. Haragan was too happy to curse. He just turned the carpet round in the air, looked over his shoulder and flew it backwards down towards the city to begin the next stage of his plan.

Zal screamed with anger all the way down, the medallion clenched in his hand. Since he'd formed his Citadel Guard ambition, he had been determined that death wouldn't have an easy time taking him. So he screamed and flailed his arms, trying to fly … and then plunged into very deep, very cold water. His head went under and the freezing water rushed into his nose and mouth. He surfaced, spitting and gasping for air, the chill making his heart pound. Zara was floating a few feet from him, surprised but unharmed. Rip was doggy-paddling about next to her.

They had fallen three hundred feet into a wide lake at the bottom of the crater. They had failed to see it on the way down because of the shadow cast by the palace and the volcano's rim. Light did reach down on the far side, however, touching the water and creating rippling reflections on the smooth volcanic walls. Zal and Zara both swam towards this, and floated in the light.

"It must be the emergency reservoir," said Zara, looking about her in wonder.

"Are you all right?" Zal said.

"I'm fine. Fine." Zara gazed up at the sky through the crescent gap between crater and palace wall.

"The emergency reservoir?"

"Yes. You've never heard the stories? The Caliph's great-great-grandfather was an obsessive butterfly collector. He once fell down a dry well while chasing a golden moisture tail. It was three days before he was found and rescued. He spent the rest of his life terrified of dying of thirst, or of anyone else in Azamed doing the same. So he started storing water for if the wells in the city ever dried up. An emergency supply. This must be it."

"Amazing," said Zal. "And I can't believe our luck." He looked up at the walls of the crater. They were coated with volcanic glass, near smooth and frictionless with no obvious handholds. He didn't notice when the water behind them shivered.

"How are we going to get out of here?" he said. "Can you use your magic?"

"Not to get us out," said Zara, scratching Rip's head. "It's too high to levitate, and I couldn't carry you and Rip. But I can use telepathy to call for help."

"Great," said Zal. "Well, do it and let's get out of here."

Zara looked at him with contempt. "Have you forgotten why we're down here?"

"Haragan pushed us…"

"We're looking for the secret of the rainbow carpet, you moron."

"We're not going to find it floating in an underground reservoir!" Zal argued.

"No, but over there looks promising."

Zara pointed ahead and to their left, where the water lapped at the mouth of a cave. Stone steps, identical to the ones Haragan had crumbled from beneath them, led up into darkness.

"Now, hold on. They could lead anywhere. We could end up in more trouble than we're in now."

"I think we're doing OK at the moment," said Zara. "Haragan thinks we're dead. He's not going to bother chasing us any more. We can weave the carpet back at your place with no—"

The still water in front of them suddenly exploded upwards, drenching them in white foam. A blue-scaled, forty-foot water dragon, as thick as a tree trunk, reared up from the depths. It vented a high-pitched, furious scream that stung their ears and shook their bones.

"AAAAAARGHH!" they screamed in unison. Even Rip joined in. Then the trio struck forward and swam as hard and fast as they could towards the cave mouth. To Zal it now looked as inviting as a warm feather bed. The water dragon roared again and breathed a huge cloud of ice shards, each as long and sharp as a spear. They rained down into the water around Zal and Zara, fortunately all missing their targets.

"Swim!" Zal and Zara shouted to each other.

The dragon hissed in anger and dived down at them, its jaws wide open. It fell short by about an inch and the wave created by its head hitting the water lifted Zal, Zara and Rip, sweeping them forward into the cave. They scrambled up the first few steps on their hands and knees, and then they were up and running for their lives.

The stairs only led up a short distance before becoming a long narrow corridor and then another staircase that led down into the cold heart of the mountain. They skidded to a stop on the first landing they came to. Zal and Zara collapsed side by side and hugged each other, trembling as they caught their breath. Rip stretched out on the floor and panted.

"I … didn't think … they could grow … that big," said Zara. Water dragons were usually the size of cats. In Azamed they were expensive, exotic pets. The very wealthy liked to have two or three swimming in the fountains of their gardens, where they could rear up out of the water and hiss at visitors.

"You were wrong," said Zal. He looked around. "Where are we now?"

They seemed to be in a larger space than they had realized. The landing was the entrance to a deep, low-roofed cave dripping with sharp stalactites, while the stairs continued off to the right, down to another landing. Zal stood up and stumbled over to the low balcony wall. He looked over.

"Creator within us!"

Zara hurried after him, looked and gasped. Rip jumped up too, resting his front paws on the ledge. His eyes widened.

The cave seemed to be bottomless. They were at the top, which was relatively narrow, but it widened as it went down. A city had been carved into its walls. Hundreds of doors and windows led off it. Stairs criss-crossed back and forth, connecting the landings and levels and the sides of the cave. Strange channels were cut into the walls, almost like aqueducts, and all of a sudden, Zal understood their purpose. The city was so ancient, it must have existed when the volcano was active. The channels controlled the lava, preventing it from destroying the city. But the cave wasn't open to the sky, and he could tell it never had been. They must have harnessed the lava, turning it to their use for heat and light. But whoever "they" were, they were long gone, Zal could tell in an instant. The city beneath them was dead. Cities had their own distinctive smells: Azamed was always alive with the scents of flowers and spices. The cold air from this city smelt of dust.

"You were right," he said.

"Hmm?" said Zara, tearing her eyes from the incredible sight below.

"This does look a promising place to find the secret. The legends must be true."

"Which legends?"

"That Azamed was built on the ruins of an even more ancient city. This has got to be it."

Zal led the way down the next section of stairs, and the next, and the next. They peered into the carved stone rooms as they went. Aside from thick dust, all were empty. There was no furniture, no belongings, not one single object left anywhere. Rip tried to go inside one but shot out again as he disturbed a large family of bats, who fluttered around them for a moment and then flew up into the cavern roof and vanished from sight. Along the landings were occasional breaks in the balcony wall – gaps a few feet wide that had definitely been built for a purpose.

"We're getting warmer," said Zara as they passed one.

"How do you mean?"

"These would have been where they launched their carpets from. They'd have needed carpets in here to get up and down the levels. Quicker than walking."

They continued their downward journey for nearly an hour. As they went they talked, discussing what they would like to do to Haragan when they finally escaped. Eventually they came to a large semi-circular balcony that occupied almost half of the shaft. In the middle of the flat side stood an ancient stone podium.

"Someone would make speeches, standing there," said Zara, her eyes distant as she imagined the scene, centuries ago. She pointed up at the three levels of balconies on the other wall. "People would stand on those to listen. And when there wasn't any space left, they'd hover on carpets."

"Rainbow carpets!" said Zal, with sudden triumph and amazement, pointing at the curved wall behind the balcony. There was a pair of double stone doors in a doorway lavished with carvings. Etched onto the doors themselves were impressions of carpets. There were no colours, but each had seven clear patterns defined on it.

"I think we've found what we're looking for," said Zal.

"I think you're right!"

Rip yapped, sensing their joy. The trio rushed forward, laughing, to push open the doors. What Zal had failed to notice was the carvings on each side of the door. These were fainter, of human figures clad in armour and carrying weapons. Just as Zal's hand touched the door, another hand shot out from nowhere and seized his wrist. The hand was strong, but withered. The skin was yellow and cracked like old parchment and was shrunken to the hand's bones. Zal's eyes moved up the withered arm and body to the almost skeletal, eyeless face.

"YAAAAAH!" He screamed and twisted against the mummy's grip but its hold on him was too tight. As Zal flailed, he registered in a dim, non-terrified part of his mind that another mummy had appeared and was holding Zara. She threw out a spell, but a line of strange symbols carved on the mummy's breastplate suddenly glowed gold. They were protection runes and the magic splashed harmlessly off the metal. Zal looked behind his own attacker and understood. The mummies were the carvings. They had been standing in alcoves on each side of the doors. The way the grey dust poured in torrents off his attacker showed they must have been waiting there for centuries.

"Gouftarn? Karlial gouftarn?" the mummy guard holding Zara demanded. The expressionless hole that was its mouth had dry skin and small, stretched lips. Zara shuddered at the sight of the cracked yellow teeth and dry shrivelled tongue as it opened and closed.

"We don't speak your language!" Zal shouted as he struggled to get free. He reached for his sword, but the mummy had already removed it without him noticing.

The guards turned to face the doors. While they could move their arms quickly, their half mummified legs left something to be desired. Turning ninety degrees took them almost thirty seconds of slow shuffling, Zal and Zara stumbling round with them. Rip, who had hung back terrified, now leapt at the mummy holding Zal. Without looking, the guard caught the yapping dog under his free arm. Rip tore a chunk out of the forearm with his teeth, exposing grey bone. The mummy did not even flinch. Rip spat out the dead flesh, repulsed by the taste.

With the grind of stone on stone, the doors

opened under their own power. The mummies shuffled forward, their rusted armour clattering. Zal and Zara were led into a long, low-ceilinged room with a carved stone throne at the far end. More mummies, eighteen in total, prised themselves out of their wall alcoves and stood to attention in two lines. Zal and Zara were pulled down between the lines to stand before the throne.

For a long moment, nothing happened. Zal and Zara looked at each other. Then, suddenly, smoke and dust exploded from the throne in a cloud of wind that almost swept them backwards. Huge, leering eyes and a mouth full of teeth appeared at the centre of it, glowing bright blue.

"YAAAAAH!" Zal and Zara screamed.

"Mallaka!" the ghost roared, silencing them. "Distinine barfourrow calchenche…"

"We don't speak your language!"

The cloud suddenly vanished and the ghost could be seen clearly. He had obviously died an old man and had a long beard trailing down to his feet. His crown was made of mist, like the rest of him. His small eyes regarded the trembling Zal and quaking Zara with fury.

"Gods!" His voice filled the room and echoed up and down the city cavern outside. "Do you condemn me such that the enemy must finally penetrate my capital? And I must address them in their own barbaric tongue! Why have I, Faradeen, the Eight Hundred and Thirty-fourth Emperor of Nygel, been forsaken? Why? *Why?*"

Indigo

There was no answer other than the echoes of the ghost's own words. They faded, and then there was silence save for Zal, Zara and Rip's breathing. The Emperor and his guards did not need to.

"Um ... Emperor?" Zara said. "I don't think... We're not your enemies."

"Not my enemies?" The ghost looked at her in scorn. "Who else are you apt to be? The enemy surrounds the Fire City on all sides, in every direction, for thousands of miles! Every province of my empire has fallen into their accursed, thieving hands. They even have the impudence to build homes and raise families on the mountainside above us! Hah! But whatever they build will be pitiful compared to the glory my Fire City once had."

The Emperor's mist eyes roamed around the dusty grey room, taking in the dry lava channels. Then he looked back to Zal and Zara.

"They send children now, do they? Is there no limit to your master's conniving and scheming? Damn the Asameedians to the glaciers and ice plains of hell!"

Zal and Zara looked at each other in concern at the name of the Emperor's enemy. Asameed was what the first Caliph, Az the First, had called his city, deciding it would be too arrogant to name it after himself. This merely made "Azamed" all the more memorable, and it completely supplanted Asameed within a few years. Legend had it that the Caliph had still been demanding the correct pronunciation on his deathbed.

"So," said the Emperor. "If you are not my enemy, who do you claim to serve?"

"Um, well…" Zal opened his hands in a gesture of apology. Haragan's medallion, which he had forgotten he still held, slipped from his palm and landed on the floor between the Emperor's feet.

"AHA!" The Emperor stood bolt upright,

pointing at it in triumph. "I knew it! The crest of Salladan Shadow! May he be crushed in a thousand freezing avalanches for all eternity!"

Zal and Zara started and looked at each other.

"The founder of the Shadow Society..." Zara murmured.

"Whatever he founded is irrelevant!" the Emperor cried. "His greatest 'triumph' will for ever be the destruction of my Fire City! The mountain was impregnable. Your masters from Asameed threw troops in their thousands against its rock walls, but not one of them broke through. Not one! The body of Nygel died, yes. But the heart beat here, in the Fire City. It still does! Asameed's barbaric Caliph knew he would never win a true victory while the city lived. So Salladan Shadow resorted to the lowest, dirtiest, filthiest tactic his vile mind could concoct!"

"What did he do?" Zal asked.

"Don't pretend ignorance to me, *spy*!" the Emperor cried, but he answered anyway. "He crept into the city, alone, in the dead of night – though night never truly came to the Fire City. He crept down to the lowest level, *and he used his pagan magic to extinguish the volcano's fire!*"

The Emperor was panting without breathing. Zal and Zara both watched him, wide-eyed. He drifted back down into his throne.

"He extinguished it and his bodyguards built the accursed maze in a single night. That gave the Caliph his victory. My people proved themselves to be weak, disloyal cowards. They minded not the mountain when we had heat and light, but when cold and dark, save for candles, they claimed they could not stand it. They left! To join the enemy on the surface. They said the war was lost, but I proved them wrong. Look at me now! I died for life everlasting. I stained my hands with the blood of my own children so that I would never be pulled to the other side – and to this day, I rule Nygel!"

The Emperor gestured at the mummies with a ghostly arm.

"My palace guards saw that. They followed me down this path so that Nygel would never fall. They were mummified alive, making no sound as their organs were drawn from their bodies and their eyes plucked out. Such is their discipline. Gods! Why could you accursed Asameedians not be content? You were primitive tribesmen. Savages. Wasting yourselves in farming and hunting. Your rightful role was as the slaves of Nygel! We gave you hovels and water and rotten bread – what more did you require? Why did you have to rebel? Why?"

"Emperor," said Zara. "This is it! This room. You and your guards. They're all that's left of Nygel. The city is dead. And … that I know of … no one, on the surface, even remembers Nygel…"

Zara leant back as she finished, expecting another screaming outburst from the ancient, hopelessly mad ghost. But the Emperor didn't scream. He gripped the arms of his throne and leant forward to look her in the eye.

"Nygel has existed since the forests that died to form the Great Desert were nothing but earth themselves. My ancestors tunnelled their way into this mountain, harnessed its fire and built on it the greatest empire the world has ever seen. Nygel's heart still beats here. Nygel exists, girl. And it will exist, and I will rule it, long after the mountain has once again become level with the sea."

The Emperor's voice rose again and he quickly regained his former tone.

"But that isn't why you two spies are here! I know

why you're here. You have come for one of two reasons. To assassinate me—"

"No!"

"Then it is the other! You have come to steal Nygel's greatest secret. The one thing that none of my deserting citizens could reveal."

"No…"

"You have come to steal the secret of the rainbow carpets!"

There was an awkward pause. Zal and Zara looked at each other and then at the floor.

"I knew it!" said the Emperor, pointing a triumphant finger at their uncomfortable faces. "You have come for the secret. Now" – he sat back on his throne and stroked his beard – "how should I punish you for that?"

Zal opened his mouth to suggest a slap on the wrist, but Zara shushed him.

"You're fortunate that I rule from beyond the grave," said the Emperor, considering the options. "I cannot pick up my favourite disembowelling knives any more. My guards don't have the muscles needed to work the rack."

The mummies hung their heads in shame.

"And we have no thumb screws, itching powder or boiling oil. So I think I will do something completely different. I will give you a chance to learn the secret! You have come closer than any of Shadow's other agents ever have. I think you deserve it."

"Well… Thank you, Emperor … of our enemy!" said Zara. "Give us this chance and we will succeed."

"For our master's glory!" Zal added with enthusiasm.

"*You* will not, girl," said the Emperor. He pointed to Zal. "It will be down to him."

Zal was outraged by Zara's horrified expression.

"Now, wait a moment, Emperor," Zara said.

"Can you fence, girl? Do you know the first thing about sword-fighting?"

"Well … maybe the *first* thing…"

"That will not be good enough. He, however, clearly knows a great deal. That scimitar has been drawn often, and I can see the calluses of practice on his hands. Come! To the chamber!"

The Emperor floated off his throne, cackling with evil and madness. Another of the mummies shuffled forward and pushed the throne aside. It was a sliding door to a small room, into which Zara, Zal and Rip were thrust. The Emperor glided after them, his misty form filling the doorway.

"Do you recognize it, boy?"

"Yes," said Zal, gulping, "I do."

Carved on the opposite wall were three deep grooves. They crossed over a centre point to form a six-pointed star.

"Then I will leave you to it," said the Emperor. "The secret will be yours when you have performed the perfect cuts. Once you have opened the second chamber, you will see a bell inside. Ring it and I will let you out. Take as long as you want. Centuries, even. Farewell and give my regards to the maggots…"

The Emperor's laughter stirred up more dust as the throne was slid back into place. For a moment, the trio were plunged into complete darkness. Zara cupped her hands and conjured up the ghosts of several thousand fireflies. They danced around the ceiling of the chamber, shedding warm, golden light downwards. Zal looked at the carving with a glum expression.

"What *is* this?" asked Zara, as Rip began leaping up at the phantom fireflies.

"Well," said Zal, "that wall is another door to another chamber – which, I presume, contains the secret. The carving is the lock. It's also an ancient sword exercise, which I have to do just right in order to open it."

"Again, what is it?"

"The six perfect cuts." Zal demonstrated with his finger. He traced each of the lines in turn, twice, once from each end, going round the circle. "I have to swing my sword through each one like that. It must not touch the stone, nor even be more than a hair's-breadth from the stone. If I do that through each groove, in the correct order, with no long pauses between each one, the door will open."

"Can you do it?" said Zara.

"I'm going to try." Zal drew his scimitar and shook his arms to loosen the muscles. "But this is an exercise you start practising when you've studied the sword for twenty years. I've done five. And it's meant to take fifty years to master."

Zal took a breath and swung his scimitar at the first groove. There was the chink of metal on stone.

"If I make a mistake, I have to start again."

Zal started again. There was another chink.

"And the race begins tomorrow morning."

Zara sat down on the floor to wait.

In the living city above the dead one in the mountain, it was late afternoon. The sky was turning orange-gold as the sun began to think about setting. Haragan, Shar and Dari were crouched on the roof of the palace. Their brown clothes made a stark contrast to the palace's light colours, but as they were at the highest point of Azamed, no one could see them. It was a serious breach of etiquette to fly carpets higher than the palace roof.

There were several skylights in the roof. As Dari worked on the lock of one of them and Shar kept watch, Haragan wandered around, looking through the others. Before coming here, he had giggled to see Augur Thesa and Arna Aura rushing through the streets searching for their missing children. But now, the sight of the Caliph's treasure room from above made him want to laugh aloud. Gold coins and statuettes and jewellery were piled up in glittering millions. When he wasn't faced with the Leader's irritating test, Haragan loved gold.

He found himself again slipping into memory,

this time a more pleasant experience: the early training sessions of the Society. They had taught him combat, magic, stealth and cunning, and he had enjoyed them. There would be mazes or trap-filled rooms, where a puzzle had to be solved for escape to be possible. The solution would always be gold: a bag just heavy enough to place on the scales to open the door; a lock for which a single gold coin was the key. It was a fantastic system which taught the young Shadows the true value of gold. It was the Cosmos Vulture's greatest gift to men; a means to achieve anything.

But Haragan wasn't here to raid the wondrous, glistening horde. The Caliph's treasure was far too vast to be carried away. It could stay where it was, waiting for the inevitable day when a Shadow sat on the throne of Azamed.

"Aha!" called Dari as the window lock sprang open.

After two hours, Zal had to change sword-hands. He was making some progress: his blade swept through the first and second grooves just as it needed to. It was when he tried for the third that the chink came.

"Will you stop sighing!" he said to Zara.

"I'm sorry. I'm just bored and tired." She was still sitting, leaning with her back against the throne.

"I'm trying my best!"

"I know. I wasn't criticizing you. It's been a frustrating day."

Zal thought about it and nodded. His blade chinked against the stone.

"So, how is it that you know Haragan?"

"He's the bane of my life," said Zara.

"I thought *I* was."

"Don't flatter yourself."

Zara gave a short laugh as she recalled their first encounter. There was bitterness in her words.

"I first met him five years ago – it was my first contest in the Under 10s. He was the Shadow Society's champion and I was the Guild's from the Under 7s. It was about halfway through the contest, and he was winning hands down, when I spotted that he was cheating."

"Oh, old habit of his, is it?" said Zal.

"He was using Tremor spells: making the ground move under his opponent's feet to distract them. It wasn't technically against the rules, but he was making them invisible and that was unfair. Every spell is meant to be visible so that the opponent can see it coming and has a fighting chance. What Haragan was doing was just sneaky."

Zal nodded. Fencing contests had similar rules. You couldn't ignore an attack made by your opponent to launch one of your own. You had to defend the attack before you counter-attacked.

"So what happened? Did you report him?"

"I wanted to," said Zara, "but I couldn't prove he had done it. I didn't know how to capture spell evidence back then. And you know how good Shadows are at denying stuff."

"What did you do?"

"The only thing I could think of. I cheated too."

Zal stopped, turned and looked at her with wide eyes.

"All I did was jump," said Zara defensively. "I jumped above the spell when he used it, and won with my next spell. Everyone saw what I did. Haragan saw me jump and he saw the spell coming. He had a chance to stop me, but I think he was too surprised."

"Sorry." Zal turned back to the wall. "I didn't think you would sink to his level."

"Actually, I did," said Zara. "I do. That match started something. Like a vendetta between us. Whenever we enter the same competition, we always end up fighting each other in the final round. Each time we do it, he's dreamt up a load of new cheats and tricks to use against me and I have to do the same. I have to spend weeks before every contest working late, coming up with new ways of cheating. Between us, we could write a book of competition cheats. And it's not easy. I have to trawl through all the records of past contests looking for inspiration. I can never do the same thing twice. I can't use anything too obvious, or anything too complex, because it all has to be fast. And we both have to worry about the judges catching us at it. It's really hard and it's exhausting, but it's better than letting him win when he doesn't deserve to, and knowing that I could have stopped him."

"You've never struck me as a natural cheater," said Zal. "But that's really why you want to weave a rainbow carpet, isn't it. Just to be sure he doesn't win."

"It's also because I don't want you and your father living on the streets," Zara said, jumping up. "It's not about Haragan and it's not because we're engaged.

You're a stupid, hot-headed camelpat, but you're OK really. I want to help you. And I couldn't bare the thought of Rip starving in a gutter."

She bent down and began tickling Rip, who rolled about in pleasure.

"All right, that was a bit unfair of me," said Zal. "You may be an arrogant, magically gifted chip in the beak of the Celestial Stork, but you're good company. I've always liked visiting Mum when you're there."

"Really?" Zara looked up.

Zal and Zara's mothers had been the best of friends. They had both died in a plague that had ravaged Azamed when the children were very young, and they were buried close to one another in Azamed's cemetery. Throughout the children's lives, Augur and Arna had taken them once a month to visit their mothers' graves. Quite often, the two families met there.

"Yes," said Zal. He shrugged his shoulders.

"I like it too," Zara said. She sat down again. "Do you ever wonder if our dads arrange it? Timing it so we would keep meeting there? Hoping it would help us fall in…"

"Oh, definitely," said Zal. His sword scraped in the second groove. "I don't think they'd put up with the amount of arguing we do otherwise."

"But we've had fun in the park by the cemetery, haven't we? Remember that time we spent all afternoon chasing that sunfire butterfly that neither of us could catch? I guess you're not bad company either."

"Thanks," said Zal. "And you'd better get used to me." His sword clinked on the stone of the third cut. "At this rate, we should be in time for next year's race."

"I think we'll have died before then," said Zara, looking around the small bare chamber.

"Can't you magic food for us or something?"

"That's it!" Zara jumped to her feet in excitement. "You're a genius, Zal!"

"Thank you," said Zal, still concentrating on the wall. "So you can do it? We won't starve?"

"Not that, you moron! You need to make six perfect cuts, right?"

"Yes, that *is* what I've been trying to do for the last two hours."

"So, I'm going to use magic to help."

Zal looked at her suspiciously.

"How?"

Zara pushed him aside and began running her hands over the carving. Blue magic glowed beneath her fingers.

"Right. I'm ready."

She stepped aside and pushed Zal in front of the carving. Standing behind him, she rested her hands on his shoulders, but Zal flinched away.

"What are you doing?" he said.

"I'm using magic to help."

"No, I mean what *exactly* are you doing?"

"I'm going to guide your sword-arm and the blade. It's a simple spell. Come on."

Zal hesitated. The legends and cautionary tales in Azamed made it very clear that magic was best left to magicians, who knew what they were doing. There were always lots of things that could go wrong. A spell to warm up the tea could bring a wall tumbling down. A growth enchantment could turn a vegetable patch into a rainforest. He thought of all the things he'd heard of people being turned into by mistake. Antelopes, butterflies, water dragons; the list was endless. And only a few of them, maybe the desert ape, could he imagine being any good at fencing.

"Zara, I'm not sure about…"

"Come on," she said. "Nothing bad will happen. I can control my magic. I won't turn you into a dung-beetle or anything."

"A dung-beetle!"

"It happened to Hani once, but I know what he did wrong. And this isn't even a transformation spell."

Zal still hesitated. He wanted to get the door open, but despite Zara's words, the risk seemed tremendous – as huge as a mountain. And even if it did work, was that how he wanted to say he had completed the six cuts? With the help of magic?

But… He was not doing this for himself. He and Zara weren't trying to find the secret so they could win the race. They weren't trying to find it so they could laugh in Haragan's face. They were trying to save Dad from ruin. And that made it worth the risk.

He turned back towards the carving.

"All right. Let's do it."

Zara placed her hands back on his shoulders and

closed her eyes. A hazy green mist appeared and swirled around Zal's arms.

"Whoa!" he said, stepping back.

"Trust me," said Zara. "Start when you're ready."

"Trust you? Earlier you took my legs…"

As the mist settled round Zal's forearms, it was as if they were glowing. There was no pain, just a strange tingling sensation, and Zal realized this was what magicians must feel when they cast their magic. He raised his scimitar, took a deep breath and swung. The tingling was still there, but it didn't seem to affect his arm at all. The air whispered as the blade sliced through the first crack as smoothly and easily as a cloth on glass. It didn't touch the stone. The magic was working! Zal smiled, reversed his grip and brought the blade back up through the second groove. By the fourth cut, his smile had become a beam. The fifth was perfect. He raised the blade for the sixth and almost hesitated, but brought it down. He stopped breathing as the tip of the blade entered the groove. It passed through without a sound.

"Drat!" said Zara. "Sorry. Let's start again. Slow it down this time."

"What?"

"You moved too fast. I couldn't cast magic at the same pace. Let's try—"

"No, you don't understand. I did it," said Zal.

"You just tried for two hours without managing to do it," said Zara, "and this door is still most definitely clo—"

Stone shrieked against stone as the door moved. Black dust billowed out from the cracks. Zal, Zara and Rip staggered back, choking, as the age-old door opened.

"I ... did it!" Zal coughed, waving away the dust.

Zara deliberately continued coughing for far longer than she needed to, to avoid answering. Finally she gave up and grudgingly spoke. "Well done."

Zal was laughing, far too elated to care. He'd done it! The hardest sword exercise ever and he had done it without help. He felt he could do it again: ten thousand times over! He'd ace the Guard entrance trials.

Rip howled with delight and the pair petted him and brushed the dust out of his fur.

"Right then," said Zara. "Let's see what the secret is."

*   *   *

"Spiders?" said Zal. *"Spiders?"*

Zara had conjured up a small tornado, which sucked all the dust out of the air and down into one corner of the first chamber. The trio now stood peering through the door to the second chamber. It was the same size as the first, but older – far older. Less skilled hands than those that had made the throne room had carved it out of the rock. The gashes and scars of chisels were still visible in the rough walls.

The room was hung with a matrix of thick spiders' webs woven in and out of each other, horizontal, vertical and every angle in between. Only a few touched the walls; most were spun between the others, and the assembly looked ready to collapse at any moment under its own weight. The webs were dotted with dozens of black spiders, about the size of human hands, each creeping leisurely about on its eight hairy legs.

"I don't understand," said Zal. He took a cautious step through the door but did not go any further. "How is this the secret?"

"I don't know," Zara said, leaning past him to look into the room. "It doesn't make any sense. After you."

"Sorry. Where are my manners?" Zal stepped aside. "You go first."

"No, please..."

"I insist..."

Rip settled it by running between their legs and into the chamber. Zal and Zara both shrugged and walked in together with great care, ducking and twisting round the sticky webs. Zara summoned through some of her magic fireflies to give them light, and a few got caught in the webs. They watched as the spiders scurried over to devour them in three or four bites of their black jaws.

"Watch where you put your hands."

"You don't have to tell me that, Zal."

They looked around. Aside from the webs, the walls of the chamber were bare of decoration. A broken, dusty spinning-wheel stood in one corner. Zal weaved his way over to examine it.

Rip scurried past him under the webs to the corner of the chamber behind the wheel. He yapped in excitement.

"What is it, boy?"

Careful of the webs, Zal crept over and moved the creaking wheel to one side. He knelt down before

Rip's discovery: a jumbled pile of empty thread spools. Short, plain wooden sticks – the kind that carpet wool was wound round.

"What's so special about those?" Zara knelt down next to him.

"I don't know. This doesn't make any..." Zal picked up one of the spools. "Wait a moment..." He felt round the stick with his fingers. Then he appeared to pinch thin air between his thumb and forefinger and draw his hands apart as if unrolling a length of wool from the spool.

"What are you..." Zara broke off as she realized that while she couldn't see anything on the spool, or between Zal's hands, she could see the shadow of a thread on the wall between the shadows of his hands. She reached out, and although there was nothing to see, she could feel wire-thin thread stretched in the air.

"It's transparent thread!" exclaimed Zal. "Invisible thread! Nygel's weavers must have made it from the web of the spiders. I understand now. It's all seven of the colours and, at the same time, none of them!"

"Like if you shine different-coloured lights together you always get white?"

"Yes. That's why I could feel it in Qwinton's fragment but not see it. And it's not magical, so you couldn't either. This is it. This is the secret. This …"

"… is what will make our rainbow carpet," Zara finished.

They gathered up the spools, two dozen of them, and stuffed them into their pockets.

"Will this be enough?" Zara asked.

"More than enough. Much, much more," Zal said. "I could weave a dozen carpets with these."

"Maybe you should."

"Should I?"

"I know you don't like weaving. But even if we win the race, your father will still need a boost to get business going again. A few flying rainbow carpets in the window…"

"We'd be rich," said Zal – and then, with more enthusiasm, "we *will* be rich!"

"Thank you, I'll be very happy to put the magic in for you. Now, let's get out of here."

They crawled out from under the webs, stood up and found the bell on the back of the door to the previous chamber.

"About how we get past the Emperor…" said Zal.

"Are you thinking what I'm thinking?"

"I think so," said Zara. "And I'll take care of the mummies."

Zal called Rip to heel and then rang the jangling bell. Within seconds, the throne slid aside and the Emperor was before them. Rage and disbelief filled his face.

"How...?"

Zal and Zara jumped straight through the ghost before he could finish. It gave the unpleasant sensation of running through an ice-cold waterfall, but they barely noticed. The mummified guards lurched forward to stop them. Zal drew his sword and clashed with three of them at once. Their ancient, rusty spearheads held, but the wood of the spear shafts was aged and hollowed by woodworm and it snapped and shattered, to their great surprise. Zara summoned her tornado back into being and hurled it at the mummies, who flew into the air and crashed against the walls of the throne room. Zal and Zara hopped, skipped and jumped over the sprawling mummies and were out through the door in seconds.

"Bye!" Zal shouted over his shoulder. "Got a race to win!"

They raced down the stairs, deeper and deeper into the mountain, laughing and congratulating each other all the way. Rip jumped and barked alongside them, prancing along in pure joy.

Their voices echoed up and down the volcano shaft, far louder than the Emperor's had. In the crater, the water dragon raised its head, listening to the faint sound. Above, on the palace roof, Shar hoisted himself back through the skylight and paused as it reached him too. Deciding he'd imagined it, he moved aside for Dari and Haragan.

The Fire City below the Emperor's throne room was as ruinous and filled with shadows as the upper levels had been, but Zal and Zara were no longer scared. They almost danced down the stairways, and when the bats, disturbed by their noise, fluttered out of the houses, Rip jumped up at them without fear.

"We've done it!"

"Didn't I tell you all along?"

"Shut up."

Zara laughed and summoned more magic fireflies, which wove and spiralled around them as they continued their long descent into the oldest part of the Fire City.

"You know, Zara, despite all the danger—"

"Zal!" said Zara, interrupting him.

Zal stopped. Zara had paused and was looking over the stone banister. He joined her and exclaimed in amazement. Spread out below them was a maze. High stone walls turned at sharp right angles, splitting and branching off and doubling back on themselves. The tops of the walls were coated with dust and the passages between them were concealed by shadows.

"Ah," said Zara. "It made no sense when the Emperor said it. But now…"

"The maze Salladan Shadow's bodyguards built in one night!" finished Zal. He surveyed its geometric twists and turns. "How, by the Stork, are we going to get through it?"

"Not a problem." Zara made the cloud of fireflies spiral around her. "Since that day Dad got us lost in the market, I've learnt loads of path-finding spells. We'll be through it in no time. Now, let's get down there."

They turned to continue downwards but then paused. The next landing ran straight across the shaft above the maze, but instead of leading to more stairs it ran straight into the wall and stopped there.

"Drat!"

Zal and Zara walked forward, peering over both sides of the final landing, but there were no more stairs below them. Zal reached the end and began examining the wall.

"The stairs can't have collapsed," said Zara. "No one's been down here for thousands of years. Who would have moved the rubble?"

"I don't think there are stairs," said Zal. He slapped the stone banister. "I think this landing is a lift."

"A lift?"

"Yep," said Zal. "I think I need to pull this lever and we'll go straight down to the maze. Get that path-finding spell ready."

He took hold of the rusty metal lever that was mounted on the wall.

"Wait," said Zara.

"For what?"

Zara regarded the lever. She looked back towards the stairs and along the bridge-like landing.

"I don't know. I've got a bad feeling."

"Oh," said Zal. "So now you *are* psychic?"

During the first year of their betrothal, when they

had been experiencing the opposite of love at first sight, Zal had tried to make the best of a bad situation. Their fathers had been trying to cultivate their relationship by making them attend each other's magic and fencing competitions. For four contests in a row, Zal had begged Zara to read his opponents' minds and relay their plans to him by telepathy. Despite her many talents, Zara was not blessed with psychic powers. She had refused to help him with magic anyway, on principle, and Zal, who'd lost two of the four contests, had never quite forgiven her for it.

"No," said Zara, "It's just a normal, bad feeling."

"We all get those, and most of them turn out to be nothing," said Zal. "It's just because I've worked it out before you, isn't it?"

Rip scampered up and sniffed around the lever. They both watched, but he neither barked nor growled.

"Two against one," said Zal. He pulled on the lever and it didn't move. Using both hands, he wrenched it down.

"Zal!"

"What's the very worst that could happen? It

could turn out to be a trick or a trap or something?"

Suddenly the landing they stood on flipped upside down. In an instant it had turned over.

Gravity kicked in when they were halfway round.

Screaming and barking just as loudly as they had done falling into the crater, Zal, Zara and Rip dropped head over heels down into the maze.

Zara landed, to her surprise, on her feet. Pain exploded through her ankles and she fell over anyway. Gasping with agony, she struggled up and looked around. The tall walls towered over her. Like the Caliph's library, the top was so far away that it seemed to close in. The maze had eaten her.

Zara looked to the right and the left. The passage she stood in seemed to stretch for an equal distance in both directions.

"Zal!"

There was no answer. The fool! How could he be so hasty? First he had wanted to wage a one-man war with the Shadow Society, and now this. She should have seen it coming. She *had*! Why hadn't she leapt forward and pulled him away from that stupid lever? The sword-obsessed idiot! Distracted, Zara shaped her hands to cast the path-finding spell ... and almost fell over in shock when nothing happened. She tried again. Nothing changed. No spell appeared between her cupped palms. Zara strained, terrified. Every muscle in her body burned as she tried to push some magic out.

None came.

Zara fell back against the wall and slid to the ground. The mountain and the maze became ten times more cold and frightening than they had been before. She couldn't cast her magic. It was gone. She was powerless; she was useless. What was Zara Aura if she wasn't a magician? She wasn't like Zal, who could fence and reluctantly weave fine carpets and was a good athlete. She was talentless without her magic. What would she do? What *could* she do?

Zara's fireflies were still humming round her, but they would fade as the magic in them cooled. How could she, Zal and Rip get out of the maze without her path-finder spell? They might wander down here for years. And that was if she could find Zal. Zara jumped up and ran down the left passage at random, calling out to him and Rip. She skidded to a halt as she realized her calls gave off no echo.

Now she understood. It made perfect sense. There must be a spell, maybe several, laid over the maze. Thick, strong enchantments that stopped her voice from echoing and suppressed her magic powers. Salladan Shadow must have been far more powerful than her. Anything done with magic could be undone with magic; a blocked volcano shaft could be unblocked if the Nygellians had a strong enough magician. But not if that magician couldn't use his powers.

Zara began running again. She had to find Zal. That stupid idiot who'd got her down here might now be her only hope.

Zal also landed on his feet, as did Rip beside him, but he was too angry to notice the pain. He could not believe it. He just could not believe it! It was so unfair! Who had led him out on this crazy quest for a rainbow carpet? Zara. Who had made him sneak into the Caliph's palace? Zara. Who had eagerly suggested they follow the passage into the unknown when they'd already fallen into an underground reservoir? Zara! But when he tried being impulsive for once, taking a chance, acting and seeing what would happen, it blew up in his face. How did she get all the luck? Did she have some strange pact with the Celestial Stork, guaranteeing good fortune? Or was the Cosmos Vulture out to get him? Either way, he could not believe it!

A whimper from Rip caught his attention, and Zal knelt down and satisfied himself that his dog was shaken, but uninjured. He looked around. He was in the exact middle of a long passage, with no indication of which way to go. The walls of the maze were smooth and tall and too far apart to climb by bracing himself between them. He tapped the stone with his finger. No: jabbing his sword point into that was out as well. How was he going to find Zara? Arrogant girl. How was she going to find him? Easily, knowing her.

"OK, boy," he said to Rip. "We're on foot. ZARA!"

There was no reply and Zal noted, a little puzzled, that there was no echo either. He gestured to Rip and they trotted side by side through the maze. He picked and chose passages and junctions at random, still calling Zara's name. Rip joined in by barking. The maze floor was pure dust, and at one point Zal tried drawing a cross to mark the passage he was going down. The cross remained for an instant and then, moved by no breeze, the dust smoothed over again. Zal jumped back. There was magic in the maze. No wonder he had found no footprints. This was going to take Zara's path-finding spell thingy. Otherwise he and Rip could be going in circles in here for years. For ever! He needed Zara and her magic and he needed them now.

Zal began running flat out, and Rip matched his pace.

"Zara!"

"Wruff!" Rip skidded to a stop as they passed through one junction, and ran back to one of the other paths.

"Rip, come on. We've got to..."

Zal broke off. He watched as Rip's nose searched just above the dust.

"Wait a minute. You've found her scent?"

"Wruff, wruff!"

Zal ran back.

"Go, boy! What are you waiting for? Go!"

He sprinted after Rip through the maze. Once he had the scent, Rip did not lose it. Forward, left, right; right, left, forward, right. They now knew they were heading in the right direction and Zal ran with growing confidence. But he was still overjoyed when it happened.

"Zara!"

"Zal!"

She skidded into the passage ahead of them, dusty and shaking. They ran towards her and Zal was surprised when Zara jumped on him and hugged him tightly, trembling. It took him a second to see the tear stains on her cheeks.

"What's wrong?"

"I can't use it!" She almost wailed the words.

"Can't use what?"

"My magic!"

"Your magic?" Zal stepped back.

"Yes, magic!"

They both leant against the walls, panting.

"There's a blanket spell of some kind," Zara said. "It's lying over the whole maze. I can't use my magic in here. Oh, Stork help me, I'm useless! We're finished."

"No path-finding spell?"

"No."

"Drat." Zal looked up and down the passage, identical to all the others. "But we're not finished. There must be some other—"

"Wruff!"

Rip was at the next turning, sniffing and looking back at them.

"Rip…" said Zara thoughtfully.

"Of course!" said Zal. "Well done, boy."

They started down the passage towards the little dog.

"You think he can lead us out of here?"

"He followed your scent. I'm sure he…"

Zal broke off as they turned the corner. They both knew in an instant that Rip had found the centre of the maze. It was a square courtyard, far wider than the passages had been. On a pedestal in the centre, facing away from them, was a statue carved from shining black volcanic glass. With Rip at their heels, Zal and Zara walked round the edge of the courtyard to see it from the front. It was of a tall man, heavily armed with daggers, his face hidden behind a tightly wound scarf.

"Salladan Shadow," said Zara.

The courtyard exploded around them. Like the

rest of the maze, the floor of the courtyard was all dust. Clouds of it shot upwards as thirty-five mummies erupted out of hiding holes in the ground. Streams of dust poured off them like rainwater off rooftops.

Zal whipped out his sword, noting that not only was he outnumbered, but these mummies were in a far better condition than the Emperor's bodyguards. Muscles and tendons were still strung to their bones beneath their dried skin. They moved fast and with precision as they surrounded him and Zara and levelled their brutal, hook-tipped spears at them.

"Zal?" Zara whispered through her teeth.

"You still can't use magic?"

"Nope."

"Then grab the largest stone you can find and be ready to throw it as hard as you can."

It wouldn't do them much good, but it was better than nothing. Zara crouched and began to search the dust with her fingers.

"Karsure!"

They both started at the mummy's barked command.

"Oh, not again. We don't speak your language!" Zal raised his sword.

"What?" exclaimed the figure. "You speak my language, but not your own?"

This mummy was tall, and the others stood aside as he stomped forward. His armour was scratched and battered, but his helmet was decorative and he brandished a chipped sword rather than a spear. Zal blinked as he spotted the worn raised mark on the helmet. The Shadow Society's symbol.

"Zara," he whispered, "let me do the talking."

"What?"

"Shh! Trust me."

Zara hesitated but kept silent.

"The offer of our master is quite specific," said the mummy. "All Nygellians who wish to do so may leave the mountain by way of the maze, but no weapons may be carried out with them. Until you surrender that sword, boy, and tell me how you speak the Asameed tongue, you may not pass."

"I will carry it with me as far as I wish, soldier," Zal said. He tried to fill his voice with all the pomp and arrogance of Haragan's.

"Then you will carry it no further than where

you now stand," said the mummy, and he raised his sword. The other mummies clashed their spearheads together.

"*Zal!*" hissed Zara.

"*Quiet!*" he whispered back, then he turned to address the mummy again. "I find it hard to believe our master will be impressed by the news that my companions and I were delayed by keeping hold of our weapons."

"Our master?" said the mummy.

Zal held out Haragan's medallion. "We are also of the Society of Shadows. The loyal servants of the Cosmos Vulture!"

If the mummy had still had eyebrows, they would have shot up. As it was, he dropped to one knee, his armour clanging, and bowed low. His undead men followed suit.

"Please, forgive me…"

"Forgiven, soldier," said Zal. "We are … agents of … our illustrious master, Salladan Shadow. We would have revealed ourselves right away, but we wanted to be sure you and your men have not been addled by such a long tour of guard duty."

"No, sir agent!" the mummy said. "We are the

Society of Shadows. We have kept our wits about us."

Zara and Rip watched the conversation open-mouthed.

"Excellent," said Zal. "Then I can give you your new orders."

The mummy's head snapped up, then bowed again.

"I imagine we are the first Nygellians to have passed through here in a while?"

"Yes, sir agent."

"Well, the last ones were in fact the very last Nygellians in the Fire City."

"I remember them well," said the mummy. "One was the youngest grandson of the original architect who had been tasked with maintaining the city's structure. He wept for an hour before leaving."

"Well, the only Nygellians left in the city now are that madman, the Emperor, and his personal guards, up in the throne room," said Zal. "My companions and I have just relieved them of the secret of the rainbow carpets."

The bowed heads of every mummy now shot up. There were gasps from dried throats and withered lungs.

"Congratulations, sir agent," said the head mummy, his voice reverent.

"Oh, it was simple," said Zal. "But now that we have it, there is no need to leave the Emperor on his throne any longer. We will take the secret back to … headquarters, where our master is waiting. Take your men upstairs, soldier and … deal with the Emperor."

Zal tried to think up a more specific instruction for how to deal with a ghost, but there was no need. The head mummy sprang to his feet and snapped off a salute.

"Understood, sir agent. Ha-ha! At last, Asameed and the Society of Shadows will be truly triumphant. Follow me, men!"

The mummies hoisted their spears and ran out of the maze, armour and weapons clattering.

"Hey!" Zal shouted after them. "How do we get back to Master Salladan?"

There was a rumble and Salladan Shadow's statue moved aside, revealing steps down to another stone corridor.

"Thanks!"

Zal grabbed Zara's arm and pulled her down the

steps, with Rip leading the way.

"I can't believe it," said Zara.

"I can scarcely believe it myself," said Zal. "But I thought on my feet and it all made sense. After the maze was built, Salladan Shadow put the anti-magic spell over it, and then he mummified his guards so they would keep guarding it and stop the Nygellians digging their way to the lava by hand. But he also knew the Nygellians would want to escape once the fire was gone, so he made the tunnel for them to use."

"And only those who went peacefully, without their weapons, were allowed to use it," finished Zara. "Zal, you're brilliant!"

"Thank you. Though I feel degraded for posing as a Shadow."

"Oh, I don't know," said Zara. "I think you'd be very good at it."

"Well, with that brilliant series of lies you gave the guard at the palace, so would you. Maybe we should look into joining."

It was a ridiculous conversation and they both knew it. But after all the dangers and terrors of the day, it was a wonderful release. The tunnel was long and straight and was carpeted not with dust, but with sand. Zal scooped up a handful and smelt it. It was a mix of volcanic stone and ground diamonds and gemstones. The sand of the Great Desert. Azamed sand. They were on their way home. They raced down the tunnel, their laughter echoing behind them.

"Next time we see Haragan, we'll ask him for some application forms."

"Great! What can we put on them? Lying to the Citadel Guard. Breaking into the palace. Stealing the greatest secret of Nygel!"

"Yes! We succeeded where their founder failed. They'd have to accept us!"

"We're the perfect candidates!"

The tunnel ended and they skidded out onto the fine, powdery sand at the foot of the mountain just as the moon began to rise. The sky was blue, showing the first stars, and they savoured the cool night air after the dry dust of the dead Fire City. Zara felt a deep warm rush stir within her. Zal watched as she stretched out her hand and conjured up a small spirit galleon, entirely of sand. The evening breeze filled its sails and it swept away across the desert.

"It's back," Zara smiled.

"Great," said Zal. "Now, please tell me how, by all the names of the Creator, you expect me to weave a full-sized carpet in one night?"

Violet

An hour later, when Zal and Zara returned to the Thesa household, it was dark. They had first gone to Zara's home to collect the money she'd saved from her love potions, and then they'd visited Zal's favourite blacksmith. He had been unhappy at being disturbed, but he had been robbed by the Shadow Society in the past: once they'd explained, he'd soon found the needles they needed. They had then run round to close to every carpet shop in the city, buying wool in all seven colours and as many shades and tones as they could find.

As Zal and Zara stumbled into the house, laden down with their purchases, Augur and Arna rushed to greet them.

"WHERE HAVE YOU TWO BEEN?"

"Oh, right. Yes," said Zara.

"Sorry," said Zal.

"*Sorry?* Is that all you can say?" Augur took his son by the shoulders and shook him. "You've been gone for hours. We've been frantic!"

"I was about to start searching the wells," added Arna, waving a grappling hook on the end of a long rope.

"We thought the Shadows had killed you both!"

"They tried to," said Zara.

"They tried to?" said her father. "Holy Stork!"

"Look, we're safely home now," said Zal. "Is this really important?"

"Really important?" repeated Augur. "We thought we'd lost you! Like your mothers."

Zal and Zara both sobered at this.

"I'm sorry," Zal said, and Augur removed his hands from his tunic. "We should have sent word somehow. I'm sorry we didn't tell you what we were doing –"

"That's my fault more than his," added Zara.

"– but right now, I need you to be angry with me later. Because I have to, somehow, weave a carpet before dawn."

Augur was so surprised by this uncharacteristic statement that he almost fell over. Zal put his share of the bags down on the table and ran upstairs.

"Wait…! *What?*" said Augur. His expression changed from amazement to suspicion. "What are you up to?"

"We're weaving a rainbow carpet so that we can win the race tomorrow," said Zara. "And don't worry about the Shadows turning up – Haragan thinks he *did* kill us. Zal! Where are you going?"

"Just lay everything out on the table!" Zal shouted from upstairs. They heard a clatter of falling boxes – he seemed to be searching for something.

Zara obeyed, emptying the bags onto the table and laying out everything they'd bought.

"Is this where you've been all day? Buying wool?" said Arna.

"No, we only spent the last hour doing that," said Zara. She didn't want her father to ask about the money. Mixing love potions was a profitable, but very disreputable, activity in Azamed. "We spent the rest of the time finding out how to do it."

"Wait a moment," said Augur. "Rainbow carpet?

Rainbow carpet? You've found out how to weave a Rainbow carpet?"

"One that flies?" asked Arna, wide-eyed.

"Yes," said Zal as he appeared down the stairs carrying a spare loom that the Thesas didn't usually have space for in the workshop. "It almost killed us, but we found it. The secret is transparent wool."

He took a spool from his pocket and passed it to Augur, who examined it first with puzzlement, then astonishment.

"Holy Stork above us!" he said, and abruptly sat down.

"You can actually do it?" said Arna, peering at the thread, then at the children.

"Ask Zara," said Zal. He took another spool of the transparent wool and began to prepare the loom. He stretched the warp threads from top to bottom and the weft threads from side to side, and within minutes he had made a grid. They couldn't see it, but the moonlight through the window cast its shadow clearly on the wall. "Right," he said. "Ready. So will you finally tell me how I do this before morning?"

"Quite simple," said Zara. "I help with magic. Like I did with the six cuts."

"You failed!" said Zal.

"Well, if you can do it all by yourself," said Zara, "let's see you thread the first needle."

Zal was thrown by this, but he picked up one of the needles nonetheless, gripped a length of the invisible thread between thumb and finger, tried to thread it ... and stopped. He could see the eye of the needle, but not the thead that needed to go through it. He could tell that the length he was trying to thread was short, but not if it was straight or hanging— Wait! There was its shadow on the wall. That was straight. He tried again, lining up the two shadows. Missed.

Zara picked up the thread reel and cupped it in her hands. Blue balancing magic glowed between her fingers and flowed down the thread. It appeared, blue and shining, as if an invisible pen was tracing it in the air between her hands and Zal's.

Augur and Arna both gasped and Rip hid behind their ankles. His confidence growing, Zal tried again but still could not quite do it. He had to hold his hands tense and then that made them tremble, and...

Zara placed a hand on his shoulder and the blue magic swirled round his arm again. This time Zal could feel it working: steadying him, calming his muscles. He tried a third time and the green glowing thread went perfectly through the eye.

Zal looked from Zara to the waiting loom to the pile of transparent and multicoloured threads before it. In his mind's eye a carpet, a rainbow carpet – the rainbow carpet he could weave – began to take shape.

"Let's do it," he said.

Zara tried to recount the story of their day's adventures to their fathers, but they were too distracted by watching Zal work. They gave up before Zara had even got as far as the palace and watched in awed silence.

Once Zara had powered his arms with orange magic for speed, Zal's fingers moved in a near blur across the frame as if following dance steps they had practised for years. The carpet and its pattern seemed to flow from under his fluttering hands. At first he was a little nervous about this new freedom in his fingers, but he had become used to it before the carpet was more than an inch long. The transparent thread was the finest he had ever used and it felt strange beneath his fingertips: it was too smooth and even, unlike the others with their varying textures. He made up the pattern as he went along, using a different shade for each part but keeping the colours in clear bands running down the whole length so that it did look like a rainbow. Beneath every band lay the wonderful transparent thread.

In the end, he wove the carpet in half a night. Blinking the tiredness from his eyes, his fingers aching and blistered, he tied the knot in the end of the last tassel and stepped back to look at his work.

"Beautiful," Augur said, yawning.

"It's fantastic!" said Arna.

"My hands are never going to be the same again," said Zal.

It was a magnificent carpet. It looked more like a piece cut from a rainbow than any other carpet in existence. Zal had used the varying tones and shades of the colours with great skill, putting the darkest shades in the middle of each band and the lighter ones at the edges so that the bands seemed to merge and blend into one another. Zal had also taken inspiration from their day's journey. Four giant water dragons curled in the corners; Qwinton's pet doves fluttered in a circle in the centre. The border repeated the design of the rainbow carpet that had been carved on the doors of the Emperor's throne room and the Emperor's crown decorated the leading edge – the side that would point forward when the carpet flew. Even the Shadow Society's symbol had been included, about to be eaten by one of the water dragons.

"It's been a pretty amazing day, hasn't it?" said Zara.

"Yes," agreed Zal. "Well, over to you now…"

He took the carpet down from the frame and spread it out on the floor. Zara sat down at one end of it and, again, magic flowed from her hands. In the same way as it had taken Zal only a short time to weave the carpet, so it took Zara mere seconds to fill it with magic. They all gasped as the transparent thread lit up within the carpet, shining brighter than the sun. The magic flowed down those threads first, faster than the rest, and it reached the end before the other colours. The carpet lifted up from the floor and rippled once, straightening out the creases within itself. When it floated, it was perfect; as even and still as a plane of metal.

"Amazing," said Arna.

Rip jumped up onto the carpet before any of them. It did not move even a fraction under his weight. Zal stepped up to join him and still it did not shift.

"It's like standing on rock!"

Zara, Arna and Augur all climbed aboard. The carpet was as solid as a stone; it seemed impossible that it wasn't touching the floor. They walked around on it as well as they could, marvelling.

"It's the perfect carpet," said Augur. "That invisible thread, it channels everything together. In normal multicoloured carpets the colours don't work together, they just overlap their effects. But this one... It's perfect."

He placed his hand on his son's shoulder. "Zal, you are, without a doubt, the most brilliant weaver alive in Azamed."

"Oh, come on, Dad," said Zal. "You could have done it just as well with a bit more time."

"No, I couldn't," said Augur. "You've a much better sense of balance and precision than I've ever had. It must come from your fencing. You'll have to teach me."

"OK," said Zal. "And… Well, today has made me a bit more interested in weaving. I wouldn't mind a few more lessons in that."

"We'll begin the day after the race," Augur promised, patting his son on the shoulder and beaming.

"Ah, yes," said Zara. "Who *is* going to ride it with me tomorrow?"

"I … I think I should," said Zal. "I'd like to. I've been here at every stage in its weaving. I mean – it's my carpet."

Rip rolled his eyes, curled up on the carpet and went to sleep.

Haragan stepped back from the telescope and stroked his chin. Shar, Dari and Etan, another Shadow who'd been there on the night of the raid, waited in nervous silence. They were in an empty attic near enough to the Thesas' house for Etan's telescope to see through the front windows. Etan had spent all day watching the house and had signalled them the instant Zal and Zara returned.

"They're made of stronger stuff than I thought," said Haragan.

When he'd first heard they were still alive, a rage

equal to that of the Dark Room had stewed inside him. But now he was calm. There was no point getting angry. He already had a solution.

"We'll switch to Plan B."

It was the morning of the Great Race. Now that Zal had agreed to compete, there was not one soul in Azamed who wasn't excited by it. The sky was filled with carpets as the racing teams took last-minute practice runs, spiralling up and down around the mountain. One very daring team tried flying their carpet under the Caliph's palace, through the crater. The water dragon's jaws missed them by mere inches and they decided not to try it again.

Maps and scorecards were being snatched up as fast as they had been printed the day before. The doors to the viewing balconies were flung open as people arrived early to get the best places. Everyone was discussing the racing teams, and much money was changing hands. No one knew for certain what quality of carpet their favourites would have, but guesses were based on the previous year – and whatever rumours were drifting about. Hundreds of bets were made every minute. The city's dishonest magicians were swamped by people bribing them to place curses on rival carpets. Being dishonest, most of them pocketed the money, promised to do everything in their power, and then did nothing at all.

Behind a protective ring of Citadel Guards, immaculate in shining ceremonial armour, the palace servants were busy assembling a special viewing area for the Caliph, his family and a few select ministers who had managed to outshine all their colleagues over the last few days. On a table stood seven race trophies: one for the first carpet to cross the line and one for the first carpet of each number of colours to finish. The city air smelled of anticipation.

A tradition of the race was that the contestants did not ride their carpets to the starting line. The etiquette was to walk from your residence to the starting balcony, your team carrying its rolled-up carpet on their shoulders. This way, no one could be certain of what carpet you were racing until you reached the balcony and made a great, dramatic show of unfurling it.

The race began on the starting balcony, which was halfway up the mountain, positioned at the feet of the Caliph's stand. It was shaped like a crescent moon and was five hundred yards long, the two tips reaching out towards the desert.

Zal and Zara left the house carrying their rainbow carpet. Rip hopped back and forth between them, barking at anyone who came too close. As Augur and Arna weren't riding, they were forbidden from entering the starting area. They had left the house before dawn to get good standing spots – and to place as many bets as they could on their children.

For the first time ever on a race morning, Zal found himself wearing a grin so wide, it hurt his cheeks.

"This is so exciting!"

"I know," said Zara. "I can't wait to see Haragan's face!"

"He wears a mask all the time."

"Well, his eyes then. They're the part of the face that reveals the most anyway."

"Hey, look, there's Qwinton." Zal pointed across the wide street, lined with other racers carrying their carpets. Qwinton was in deep, anxious conversation with Captain Burs.

"Robbed! Burgled – in my own home! And they

even had the cowardice to do it while I was out. Where is the sportsmanship in *that*, Captain? Where?!"

"Sir magician, could you please calm down. You're not the only person this has happened to. Now, what…"

Zal began to turn towards them, but Zara stopped him.

"Zal! The race begins in fifteen minutes. We'll have to say hello when we're done. When we've won."

"You said it!" said Zal. "We're really going to do it, aren't we. No one is going to come close!"

"Yep," smiled Zara. "I'm expecting us to win this one and then be disqualified from next year's race because we didn't give anyone else a chance."

They reached the starting balcony.

"Thesa family team," Zal said to the magician at the gate who was registering the teams as they arrived. "Zal Thesa, Zara Aura and Rip riding a multicolour carpet."

After saving them from an eternity in the maze, there was no doubt that Rip had earned his place on the carpet.

"Right you are," said the magician, who also taught at the Guild school and had noticed Zara's absence from his lesson yesterday. "Ms Aura. That homework is still required."

"Yes, sir," said Zara as they went through the gate. "Over my dead body," she muttered as they passed out of earshot.

The magician waved his hand up at the race obelisk, which was a fifty-foot rectangle of yellow sandstone. Dust and chips of stone flew as *Thesa family. 3 riders. Multicolour*, was carved onto it by an invisible magic chisel. Zal read the other names.

"The Shadow Society isn't here yet," he said.

"Haragan's going to have a nasty shock when they arrive," Zara replied.

They walked past the carpets that were already hovering along the balcony. The race rule was that the single-colour carpets started at the tips of the crescent to give them a slight advantage, with the others further back depending on how many colours they had in them. The six-colour carpets, Zal thought, would be in the very middle. He grinned again. The one- and two-colour teams were not after the big prize: they knew they couldn't compete with any carpets containing more than four colours. These teams were seeking the runner-up prizes, to be the best carpets in their categories.

"Hi, Zara!" Hani shouted and waved from amid the single-colours.

Behind the Caliph's stand was a public balcony, almost as long as the starting one, and Augur and Arna waved their encouragement from the middle of it. The other spectators watched Zal and Zara with interest, keen to see how far along the balcony they would walk. There was no reaction as they reached the two-colours, or the three. Four-colours and above were the carpets that really made the race interesting.

As Zal and Zara passed them, there were murmurs. These became excited chatter as they entered the fives, and a lot of people announced "told you so" as they walked past even these and placed their carpet down in the very middle.

Grinning from ear to ear, Zal and Zara rolled out the carpet.

All talk was silenced. Then everybody gasped. The Caliph, who had just arrived and sat down, jumped up again. Augur and Arna congratulated themselves on raising such talented children. Zara touched the seven-colour rainbow carpet with her foot and it rose from the ground and floated, its colours shining brighter than diamonds.

The spectators breathed out and began shouting and screaming, laughing and crying. In seconds the balcony was half empty as people ran off to change their bets. The Caliph had to ask twice which team the rainbow carpet belonged to. His ministers were so shocked that no one heard him the first time.

Zal and Zara made a grand display of stepping onto the carpet and sitting down with utter nonchalance. Even Rip joined in by leaping on board and then going straight to sleep. Zal drew and polished his scimitar and Zara inspected her fingernails, both loving the envious – or even horrified – looks from the other racing teams.

"We're going to win," whispered Zal.

"So you think," said Haragan.

Zal and Zara's heads shot up. Rip growled as Haragan, Shar and Dari swaggered up, grinning beneath their scarves. They stopped beside the Thesa team. Haragan stood with crossed arms and a smug expression as Shar and Dari unfurled their carpet.

Zal and Zara's mouths dropped open. The Caliph jumped up from his throne again. Some of those changing bets snatched their money back. Augur bit his own fist to keep from screaming. Arna fainted.

At one end of the Shadow Society's racing carpet was the fragment that Qwinton had shown them. At the other was the one from the Caliph's library. A new section of carpet had been woven to connect them and make a full-sized racing carpet. Zal's weaver's eyes saw in an instant that the new section did not contain the transparent thread. There was a chance that it would not fly...

Haragan quashed Zal's hopes by reaching down and touching the carpet. It rippled and wobbled, rose and floated – albeit at an awkward, uneven angle – several inches in the air.

"You thieving, cheating camelpats!"

Zara snatched Zal's scimitar from his hand and would have leapt forward had Zal not grabbed it straight back. He clamped his hand over her mouth and spoke to Haragan. Fighting could get them disqualified.

"You stole the fragments?"

"We merely had the good fortune to find them at a street market. We have the receipts to prove it," Haragan said.

"There never is any evidence," Zal murmured.

"How do you fancy your chances now, Thesa?" Dari said. He stepped onto the carpet and stumbled as it buckled under his weight. It steadied and he sat down, but the carpet keeled to the left so that he was sitting at an angle.

"I'd still say they were pretty good." Zal released Zara, who had now calmed down. He pointed to the Shadow carpet, which was almost twisted in the air. "How much speed do you think you're going to get out of that?"

"More than enough," said Shar.

"We've got one advantage over you," Zara said.

"Oh yes?"

"Yes." Zara looked at the fragments that had once been whole rainbow carpets. The different patterns meant they must be from two different ones. "You don't know the secret. You've made that carpet fly but you don't know how you've done it. I do. We wove this one from scratch. We know the secret, and we can use it against you."

Haragan's eyebrows moved. Not very much, but it showed a slip in his confidence – which had already been shaken last night by the news that his greatest rival had somehow returned from the dead.

At that moment a bell was rung, signifying that the start was near. The Shadows mounted their carpet and it wobbled, steadied and floated still more unevenly. Zal and Zara shifted around to face forward, out towards the desert, the race landmarks and obstacles just visible in the distance. The other racing teams – the obelisk now had two hundred and thirteen names carved on it – had quick, last-minute conferences.

Zal leant forward over Zara's shoulder.

"How can we?" he whispered.

"What?"

"The transparent thread. How can we use it against them?"

"No way I know of," Zara replied. "I just said it to throw them."

"Oh," said Zal. "Right."

The bell was rung again, this time by the Caliph himself. The signal was simple: go! The carpets leapt across the starting line.

The sky around them filled with carpets. The start was the most dangerous time for collisions and most of the teams climbed, searching for the space to accelerate. Zara instead took the rainbow carpet straight forward. She wove it through the competition with the same ease with which Zal had wielded his sword and his needles. The carpet was unlike any she had ridden before; it obeyed her instructions with absolute accuracy. Most carpets, even six-colours, suffered the problem of drift – the carpet's own momentum carrying it a little bit further than intended. But the rainbow carpet had astonishing precision: it moved not a fraction further than she had intended. All the turnings were as smooth and accurate as a set square. The acceleration happened at an even pace, and Zara could sense that deceleration would never be necessary. The carpet could come to an instant stop, regardless of its speed, if she told it to.

"It's perfect!" She laughed with joy as they overtook the last five-colour team.

Zal didn't hear her. He hadn't noticed the carpet's performance: he was looking backwards, his attention fixed on the spectacle that had the Shadow Society's Leader, in his secret viewing box, jumping up and down with fury. Haragan's patchwork rainbow carpet was floating across the starting line at a speed of perhaps one centimetre per second. Shar and Dari were shouting at Haragan, who, in clear desperation, was pouring extra magic into the carpet. Zal's heart rose so fast it almost leapt. He pointed at the struggling carpet in delight.

"Ha!" he yelled, then "Whoa!" as Zara cleared the other carpets, took the lead and accelerated. The rush of speed pushed Zal forward onto his stomach and he almost slid overboard. Grasping the edge, he pushed himself back up and twisted round.

Zara grinned at him over her shoulder. "This is brilliant!"

Zal realized how fast they must be going. Usually in the race you could enjoy the fabulous scenery, but the desert around them had been reduced to a blur. The rushing air was like a hurricane blowing in one direction. Rip scrambled to the head of the carpet and barked with exhilaration, his long ears rippling back in the wind. Zal looked over his shoulder to see the city had become merely a shape in the distance.

The other carpets looked no larger than flies, so far behind.

"Ha-ha!" he yelled, and Zara echoed him.

Rip barked, and Zara peered ahead. "Zal, the cup! This is it!"

Zal glanced ahead and pulled a cup from inside his tunic. The first racing landmark was the Small Oasis, where the racers changed direction from west to south. The ritual of the cup was a racing tradition that had been started by bravado and continued by it. It gave no extra advantage, but anyone who did not do it would never sleep easy at night knowing that their run of the race had been less than perfect. Zara slowed the carpet and the desert ceased to be a blur. The oasis, a small pond of shining water with two green palm trees growing by its side, appeared ahead. Zal lay down flat on the carpet and stretched his right arm, cup in hand, over the edge. The wind whipped his tunic sleeve back and forth against his arm. Zara brought the carpet down until they were a mere foot above the ground, and they zipped past the palm trees and skimmed over the surface of the oasis, their slipstream rippling the water. Zal scooped up a cup full of clear desert water and pulled himself back into a sitting position as they wheeled round and began to fly south.

"Did you get it?"

"Yes!"

Zal drank a quick mouthful from the cup and held it before Zara's face so she could do the same. Rip turned round and Zal lowered the cup so he could lap up the last of it. The ritual completed, they sped south across the sands.

Zal sat back, feeling a joy greater than he had ever felt before. They had the best carpet. They were miles ahead in the race. Their greatest rival was probably only just out of the city...

Out of habit Zal glanced over his shoulder and, to his horror, saw the Shadow Society's carpet. Haragan's saturation with magic had worked: the carpet still rippled and wobbled as it flew, but they had caught up.

"Camelpat! It's them!" Zal yelled.

Zara looked over her shoulder, cursed and began to speed up. The Shadow carpet went low over the oasis as they performed the cup ritual and then began to climb and accelerate.

"Zara, they're catching up!"

"This is it!" Zara yelled.

"What?"

"Maximum speed! I can't get it to go any faster."

Even the rainbow carpet seemed to have its limits. Zara could feel how it was pushing through the air; the rectangular shape was holding it back and she knew that even Haragan's tactic of pouring in more magic wouldn't help at this stage.

A flaming arrow zipped past them and buried itself in the sand, extinguishing in a puff of smoke. Behind and above, Dari stood upright on the Shadows' carpet and drew the string of his longbow back to his chin. Shar reached up and ignited the oil-soaked arrow tip.

"Celestial curses!" Zal said as Dari fired.

The arrow flew down towards them, the orange flames trailing and giving it the appearance of a small burning comet. Zara steered the carpet to the left and it missed them, but Dari was already drawing the bow for his next shot.

"Yoww!" This one came close enough that Zal had to duck.

Zara was flying them in a zigzag across the desert, still at full speed, but Dari was an excellent archer.

He judged their movement, compensating for wind, and his arrows kept coming closer.

"Zara, do something!" Zal yelled.

As Zara looked around in frantic desperation, her eyes landed on Rip, who was jumping up and down and barking furiously at the pursuing carpet.

"Take over!" She scooted out of the driver's position and the carpet wobbled. Zal jumped into her place and steadied it; he was no sorcerer, but a magic carpet could always be flown by its weaver.

Zara stood gazing at the Shadows for a second and then raised her arms. Rip barked in surprise as she levitated him up off the carpet and into mid-air. His barks became terrified as she raised him higher and higher, up to the level of the Shadow carpet, and then deposited him onto it.

Surprised by his sudden appearance, Shar and Dari hesitated long enough for Rip to get his bearings, recognize his master's enemy, jump up and sink his teeth into Dari's arm. Dari dropped his bow and screamed, arms flailing.

"Shar, do something!" Haragan shouted.

Shar grabbed hold of Rip's back legs and pulled. Rip came loose but Dari had been pulling in the opposite direction and toppled backwards off the edge of the carpet. The timing was, by accident, perfect. Dari fell five feet, screaming all the way, and landed safe but winded on top of the second racing landmark, the Sky Stone, a tremendous black meteorite that had struck earth centuries ago and was now half buried in the sand. The two carpets turned east, and were travelling at such a speed that Dari was soon left far behind.

Shar realized he was still holding Rip. A phantom pain from two nights ago burned in his leg and he threw the ferocious dog overboard. Rip dropped three feet before Zara's magic caught him and guided him back down to the Thesa carpet.

"Well done, boy!" Zara laughed as she caught him.

"Zara," Zal called, "I can't drive through this!"

Zara turned. "Switch back!" she yelled, and they again swapped places.

Up ahead was the third landmark: the Mushroom Rocks. Eons of sandstorms had carved the huge boulders there into strange mushroom shapes, the smallest of which was two hundred feet tall. They looked impossible, structures that could not – or should not – truly exist. Azamed's children's stories said they had been made by some of the Celestial Stork's more playful chicks, and that the Stork herself had left them as they were because she treasured the memories. No one in the Great Race flew around them: they always flew right through the middle. It was the most treacherous and exciting stretch of the race and required the greatest piloting skill. Zal wasn't at all ashamed at asking Zara to take over – being smeared like an insect would not be a good end to the race.

With Haragan and Shar still above them and close behind, they entered the natural maze. The rainbow carpet's manoeuvrability became their lifesaver, as did Zara's quick reflexes. She steered, twisted, turned and wove the carpet through the long, dangerous path the rocks had to offer. She swung left to avoid one outcrop, dropped down to avoid a second, made a sharp right round the largest mushroom head and shot through a natural cave, grinning with exhilaration the whole way. Zal sat behind, holding tightly to Rip, his face whiter than snow.

Haragan and Shar had a more difficult time. The

ends of their carpet were free from drift due to the transparent thread, while the middle, which they'd hastily woven the night before, wasn't. It kept moving sideways, pulling the carpet out of joint. They had lots of close calls, coming near enough to the mushroom heads to reach out and touch them. They did brush several, the rough rock tearing open the threads, which Haragan had to use quick magic to repair. At last the two carpets shot out onto the golden rolling desert once again.

"Zal. Large Oasis!" Zara shouted, and Zal readied the cup again.

Haragan brought his carpet down to the Thesas' level and they skimmed across the lake of the Large Oasis almost as one. Zal and Shar both scooped up the water, but the Shadows' carpet climbed back to its menacing altitude faster and took the lead as two passengers, not three, needed to drink the water. Once the Thesa carpet had left the lake and headed north towards Arc Rock, the Shadows were ready with their next trick.

Zal watched as Haragan and Shar switched places. Standing tall at the edge of their carpet, Haragan held up a small wicker basket where Zal could see it. Zal wrapped his fingers round his sword hilt. Haragan took the lid off the basket. Out of it erupted three dozen pygmy dragons. Their wings fluttered into life and they swarmed down like hail towards the Thesa carpet, their teeth gnashing together and smoke and flames puffing from their nostrils. If Zal had possessed magic he would have sensed the enchantment they carried: an insatiable hunger for carpet thread. Haragan had sensibly enchanted his own carpet to smell unappetizing.

Zal whipped his scimitar from its scabbard. Failure did not enter his mind; it was unthinkable. He had no choice but to do it right this time. The dragons streamed downwards, and in his mind's eye they turned into multicoloured handkerchiefs falling towards his upturned face.

Zal brought up the sword and swung. He cut it back and forth in short, tight arcs, slicing the dragons out of the air before even one of them could reach the carpet. Each single one, pair, and once three in one go, Zal cut asunder. They exploded in small pops of flame and magic as the blade went through them. Zal gritted his teeth, stopped himself from blinking and ignored his burning muscles.

He saw the dragons and the handkerchiefs falling together. He cut all seven colours, and then so many more. Suddenly the air was empty and Zal returned, panting, to reality. Haragan stamped his foot and almost fell overboard as his scavenged carpet sank beneath the impact.

"Zal?" said Zara, who had been facing forward the whole time. "Did something just happen?"

Zal thought for a moment, then realized how much his arm hurt. "No," he said, and sat down.

At the same moment, Zara looked over her shoulder. "Look out!" she yelped.

Zal turned just as Haragan's carpet swooped down and came alongside them. With less than an arm's length between them, Shar swung his Burying Blade across the gap, aiming not at the riders but their carpet. Zal drew his sword and parried Shar in the same motion. Rip launched himself at the Shadow, but Shar was ready for him and whacked him aside with his free hand. The little dog skittered off the edge of the carpet, but at the last second he managed to bite into it and hold on with his teeth. Shar and Zal slashed back and forth at each other in fury, their blades sparking like fireworks as they clashed. Zal scooted round on his bottom and shot both of his feet out, across the gap, into Shar's stomach. As Shar stumbled backwards and wobbled on the edge of the Shadow carpet, Zara reached over her shoulder and fired a green magic bolt straight into his chest. He fell backwards, the carpet vanishing from under his feet, and landed in the sand dunes just as both carpets shot through the giant natural archway, as big as a cathedral door, that was called Arc Rock: the last landmark of the race.

Now began the long final stretch of desert to the finish line. Zal helped Rip back up onto the carpet and was amazed to see that his teeth hadn't damaged it in the slightest. Haragan, the last member of the Shadow team, pulled away from them lest Zal should attack his carpet with his sword. The three members of the Thesa team watched Azamed reappear in the distance, a tiny shining light on the horizon.

"We can still win," said Zal.

"We're *going* to win," Zara said.

They both looked across at Haragan, who was looking between them and the city, trying to think up new tactics.

"We're ready for you," muttered Zal.

A faint sound slipped through the wind and reached their ears. It was soft, but drawn out long enough to be noticeable. Zal, Zara and Rip all looked round, and at each other, recognizing something familiar in it. A note of triumph and madness. Haragan heard it too, and they saw him look over his shoulder and then freeze.

Another carpet was catching them up.

"That's too fast! That's not a six-colour," said Zal.

The carpet became clearer as it drew closer, and they could just pick out seven colours woven into it. But the colours had all faded almost to grey with age. There were two riders on it, together with a third shape – a kind of hazy mist that hung over its centre and didn't fade or trail out behind.

"Holy Stork!" said Zara.

The carpet drew closer still.

"AHA!" The last Emperor of Nygel pointed at them, rage and triumph in his eyes. Two mummy guards were on the carpet with him – Salladan Shadow's bodyguards had evidently tried to complete their mission. One of the mummies was missing his left arm; the other, who was driving, was missing his head.

"Left," the Emperor commanded the headless one. "That's too far. Yes, that's better. *Aha*, there you thieves are! Two rainbow carpets, woven in a single night. The audacity! You will pay for it! Your masters will not profit from it! You will pay ten thousand times! The secret of the rainbow carpets will go to the grave with you!"

Haragan looked over at the Thesa carpet, astonishment in his eyes. Zal found himself wishing they could stop and explain. The Emperor's sudden appearance was almost embarrassing.

There was a whistling sound, and Zara pulled the carpet to the right as a long, thick spear flew past them and thudded into the sand. It took Zal less than a second to recognize it. He'd seen a display of them in a dusty cabinet in Azamed's museum. An aerial javelin: a weapon designed for the Carpet Wars and used in them to great effect. The metal spearheads, which spun when thrown, were sharp and heavy; they could cut through the tightest weave of carpet in mid-air. Then the spear shafts below the heads, which were covered in metal hooks and spines, would catch the loose ends of the thread. The weight of the javelin would pull on these, unravelling the carpet from the inside, which was far more difficult to repair than the edge. One well thrown javelin could take even a rainbow carpet out of the air.

"Hold on!" Zara swung the carpet again as the mummy threw another, which missed them even more narrowly than Dari's arrows. Haragan was watching in delight and began to push ahead – until the mummy threw one at him and managed to tear off several of his carpet's trailing back tassels. The mummy then began hurling at them alternately, almost in rhythm with the Emperor's maniacal laughter. The Thesa and Shadow carpets wove and zigzagged across the sands.

"Left! Left! Left!" Zal shouted. Zara obeyed and another javelin struck the sand. Zal drew his sword but kept it at his side. He could only parry once. The javelins were thick and heavy – he could knock one of them away but it would snap his sword.

"Yikes!" Haragan was having no easier time of it, and with his crew gone he had to look over his shoulder to see the missiles coming as well as keeping the carpet on track. Where on earth had this ghost come from? No ghosts had been listed on the race obelisk; he'd read all the names before they left.

"Give me your hand," Zara called to Zal, reaching behind her.

Without thinking about it, Zal did so.

"Whoa!" Powerful red magic spiralled up his arm. The effect was far brighter and more impressive than it had been in the caves. "What did you just...?"

"Catch the next one!" Zara shouted.

"What?"

"Catch the next one!"

"Catch the next one?"

"Yes!"

"Are you insa—?"

The next javelin flew straight towards them. Its head and jagged shaft spiralled as it flew, sunlight exploding off the points and edges. Zal's enchanted arm came up faster than he could have ever moved it, even in swordplay, and caught the javelin. His hand closed on the shaft just behind the barbs and stopped the flying weapon an inch from his nose.

"Holy Stork!"

The mummy on the Emperor's carpet, and Haragan on his, both paused in amazement.

"Have you got it?" Zara called.

"What? Yes!"

"Great. Throw it back!"

"Throw it back?"

Zal looked up at the Emperor's ancient carpet, thirty feet above them and just as far behind.

"The spell..." Zara yelled.

Zal reversed the javelin, drew back his arm and threw, putting behind it every muscle he could find. The blue halo around his arm surged forward, adding the force of an avalanche to his throw. The javelin was carried up, up, higher than should be possible. The mummy guard ducked to avoid it and it passed straight through the furious, ranting Emperor.

"Curse you, insolent boy!"

"Ha-ha!" Zal jumped up and down in delight and readied himself for the mummy to throw the next javelin. It did; he caught it, spun it round and hurled it straight back.

There was a flash of magic off to Zal's left and he glanced over to see Haragan casting the same red spell on his own arm. Swivelling round, so he was flying his carpet backwards, Haragan mirrored Zal, catching and returning the javelins that came at him.

Within seconds they had a rhythm going. The mummy threw the javelin at Zal. Zal caught it and threw it back. The mummy caught it and threw it at Haragan. Haragan caught it and threw it at the mummy. The mummy caught it and threw it at Zal. One javelin went through this several times before Zara, who was watching over her shoulder, realized they were getting nowhere.

"Zal, hold the next one!" she called. "You both have to do it together!"

"What?"

"He's only got one arm. HARAGAN!"

Haragan looked over.

"Hold the next one!"

"What?" He looked at Zara in astonishment. He could barely believe she was addressing him. They were mortal enemies! Or at least they had been before she and Thesa had come back from the dead.

The mummy threw a new javelin at Zal; Zal caught it but held it by his side. The mummy waited, as if expecting Zal to return it to him. The Emperor bellowed at him and he picked up another and hurled it at Haragan. Haragan also caught it, made to throw it, then paused and looked to the Thesa carpet.

"GOOD!" Zara shouted. "Now, BOTH TOGETHER!"

Zal and Haragan looked at one another. Mistrust and suspicion filled Zal's face and Haragan's eyes.

"THROW!" Zara bellowed.

They both threw, their javelins climbing in twin arcs. The guard caught Zal's with his one arm. Haragan's speared him straight through the chest, carrying him backwards, through the Emperor and off the edge of the carpet. The mummy's body crumbled to dust and his empty armour, with its shattered breastplate, thumped on the sands.

"NO!" The Emperor shook his fists.

"Huzzah!" yelled Haragan.

"Howzat!" screamed Zal.

"Switch places!" shouted Zara. She grabbed Zal and pulled him into the driver's place as she moved out of it.

"What are you...?"

"Just drive. I'm going to finish this."

Zara stood up on the carpet, facing the Emperor, and raised both her arms. The wind whipped her head and her clothes but she stood firm and began chanting. A cloud of white magic spewed from the space between her palms and surged through the air, up towards her enemy.

"No!"

Now the Emperor's scream was of fear. All ghosts have some magical powers, and his magic now crackled alive, forming a pale grey bubble round his carpet and one remaining mummy. Zara's white mist struck the edge and pushed. The bubble bent inwards, rolled and wobbled but held intact. Zara strained and pushed harder, sweat beading on her forehead. The magic pushed the bubble in a little further, but slowly it was pushed out again.

"No..." Zara strained.

Suddenly a second, red column of magic struck and merged with Zara's first. She and Zal and Rip looked to see Haragan standing on his unbalanced carpet, adding his power to the fight.

"Both together!" Haragan shouted. This ghost and its mummies were dangerous. They had to be destroyed. Whatever it took.

The two magicians pushed. The bubble moved back in. They pushed harder and harder still, their white and red magic merging into a dazzling pink. The bubble shrank in further, crackled and finally burst. Their magic shot forward and enveloped the Emperor, the mummy and the carpet.

"NOOOOoooooo!"

Faradeen, the Eight Hundred and Thirty-fourth Emperor of Nygel, screamed for the last time as the combined spells took effect. His ghostly form, the mummy's dried body and the carpet all faded away, scattered on the winds of time. Their souls had departed at last; gone to whatever awaited them on the other side.

"Phew!" Zara turned back to Zal. "Switch back."

"Are you sure? You're OK?"

"I'm fine. Let me take over."

"All ri— Watch out!"

Haragan looked around and found he still had red magic glowing on his hands. He considered for a moment, then spun on his heel and fired.

"Whoa!" screamed Zal and Zara. There was no time for a magical block. Zara threw herself flat as Zal wrenched the carpet out of harm's way. The magic hit the top of a sand dune, churning dust into the air.

"Scoundrel!" Zal screamed across at Haragan.

Haragan, imagining the punishment the Society would mete out for his failure, didn't return the insult. "Cosmos Vulture, be with me now!" he yelled as he drew his Burying Blade … and realized, in that moment, that he did not really believe.

He again brought his carpet alongside the Thesas' and the two of them raced side by side, a few feet above the ground and almost touching. The fighting intensified to chaos. Haragan fought Zal with his dagger with his left hand and Zara with magic with his right. Zal knelt on the carpet and held Rip back with his free hand as he cut and slashed, trying to both injure Haragan and damage his carpet.

Enchantments, curses and small demons spewed from Haragan's and Zara's spell-casting hands and destroyed each other in the air between them. The magic crackled and trailed behind, giving the two carpets the appearance of one fiery comet containing all seven colours. In the city, Arna fainted again and Augur chewed his hat. The Caliph had to push several people aside for a better view.

On the carpets the conflict was reaching a stalemate. As Zal realized it, his desperation began to grow. Haragan could match him as a sword-fighter and Zara as a spell-caster. They weren't going to win. The race might even be a draw! Unless … he did something drastic.

Zal parried Haragan's dagger and pushed it upwards, out of the way, as he jumped across onto Haragan's carpet. It was an unheard-of tactic, but it worked.

Zal collided with Haragan, causing him to lean to the right. The Shadow carpet followed this movement, peeling away from the Thesa one.

"Zal!" Zara shouted in horror.

Zal pushed Haragan onto his back on the carpet and then twisted to wave Zara on. He was frantic for her to obey. It would all be for nothing if she came back for him.

"Go!" he shouted, just as Haragan punched him in the face. Zal's sword went flying off into the desert sands but he ignored it, grabbed Haragan's arms and wrestled, trying to get the dagger away from him. In glimpses he saw, to his great relief, that Zara had obeyed. Their rainbow carpet was still on course for the city and the finish line. But Rip was dancing at the carpet edge, barking at him in anguish and Zara kept looking back over her shoulder.

"Go!" he shouted again. He turned back to Haragan just as the dagger flew towards his face.

What happened next, Zal could never quite remember. He gripped Haragan's wrist to turn the strike aside and they somehow turned a double-somersault on the wavering carpet, landing on their sides. All of a sudden they were almost alongside Zara and Rip. Zal found himself on his back with Haragan over him. The Burying Blade came down. Zal rolled aside. The blade plunged through the Caliph's section of the rainbow carpet, a few inches from the back edge and buried itself, up to the hilt, in a small rock that was jutting up from the desert.

The carpet kept going and Haragan released the dagger hilt just in time not to be pulled off with it. At the same time, he and Zal saw that the dagger, buried in the rock, still had a chunk of carpet round it – which was still connected to the rest of the carpet by a long length of stretched wool. Which kept getting longer.

The Shadow Society's scavenged patchwork rainbow carpet was unravelling.

"No!" Haragan screamed.

Zal punched him in the stomach and leapt to his feet, conscious that the carpet was fast disappearing from under them. But his own, proper rainbow carpet, and his crew, were a bare ten feet away. If only he could…

Zal ran the three steps left of the Shadow carpet and launched himself across the gap.

He almost fell short. His grasping fingers gripped the waving tassels on the end of the carpet. Zal's fingers were long and thin, and years of fencing and weaving had made them strong. He held on. His legs slammed and then bounced against the desert, raising up a great trail of sand behind them.

"Zal!"

"I'm here!"

As Zal strained, Rip bit into his tunic and pulled. Zara's magic formed a soft cushion under him and he slithered forward onto the carpet. Rip barked with joy.

The twin green flags of the finishing line came into view and they all looked to the left, at Haragan, who was also holding on by his fingertips – to his last few inches of carpet. The two teams, Thesa and Shadow, were neck and neck.

Haragan's carpet ran out ten feet before the line and he thumped down on his stomach into the sand. In an explosion of cheering and a storm of falling flower petals, Zal, Zara and Rip crossed the finishing line.

Rainbow

Zal, Zara and Rip glided to a halt and stepped down from their winning carpet. They found that all they could do was jump up and down on the spot, screaming with triumph and laughter. Rip howled in excitement. Augur and Arna burst out of the cheering crowds and ran up, crying with delight, to hug their children and join the jumping and dancing.

"We did it! We did it!"

"We won."

"You won."

"You did it. You *did* it!"

"Where did that ghost come from?"

Zal sat down as the fatigue at last caught up with

him. Zara dropped beside him and said, "And, did *we* show Haragan."

"Yes, I think you did," said a voice behind them.

Zal and Zara leapt to their feet; they both knew it was the height of bad manners to sit while the Caliph was standing. He smiled and handed Zal the chest containing the prize money.

"Thank you, Your Excellency. Thank you," Zal said, trembling. He just managed to bow without falling over.

"You deserve it, my boy," said the Caliph. "Your carpet is indisputably the finest this year. All kinds of tricks from a cheater and then that ghost and it carried you through all of them. May I?"

"Of course, of course." Zal and Zara stood back as the Caliph examined their rainbow carpet with approving hands.

"Magnificent," he said, winking at them. "And I always thought rainbow carpets were just a story."

Suddenly they were all distracted by a voice shouting, "Grab him!"

Haragan, bruised and dusty, stumbled across the finishing line to be seized by two guards.

"Ha!" Zara yelled, jumping up and down. "I finally beat you. Finally. Ha!"

She stopped and blushed, remembering that there was such a thing as being a bad winner.

"What?" said Haragan. His surprise was clear as he was pulled up before the Caliph.

"You're under arrest," said Captain Burs, who had joined them.

"What?" said Haragan again.

Burs grabbed Haragan's right wrist and held it up, pulling off his glove. Glinting on Haragan's third finger was the blue-white diamond ring from the Caliph's study.

"My personal thief-detector," said the Caliph without humour. "I keep one in every room of the palace. They all carry Siren spells. No one of an impure heart is able to resist taking them. This one is from my library, and that was definitely my fragment at the tail end of your carpet. That you stole it is bad enough, but I'm insulted that you put it on the back rather than the front."

Haragan's eyes were as wide as two full moons. Zal and Zara looked at each other with amazed relief and then quickly looked forward, remembering that they knew *nothing at all* about the contents of the Caliph's private library.

"Your biggest mistake," said the Caliph, "was to forget that we in the city observe the race through telescopes and magical means for the whole duration."

"We saw every attempt at cheating made by you and your team," said Captain Burs. He turned to his deputy. "Have his teammates arrested as soon as they've walked back. And aside from cheating, theft and attempted murder, I also want to question you regarding a very suspicious fire at the Thesa residence."

"Despite helping to deal with that ghost, I cannot ignore your dangerous, illegal and *unsporting* racing tactics," the Caliph said. "The Shadow Society is hereby forbidden from ever again competing in the Great Race."

The six Secretaries for Proclamations began fighting to be the one to write this down.

"On the subject of the Shadow Society, Your Excellency," said Burs, "it occurs to me that this would be the perfect time to conduct a thorough investigation and audit of their activities. I've received many complaints about them over the years, but in this race they've stepped too far."

"An excellent idea, Captain."

The crowds, many of whom had fallen foul of the Shadow Society at one time or another, raised a mighty cheer.

Haragan let the guards lead him away without resistance, but Zal stepped up to him. They looked at each other. Zal was familiar with the tales of the Shadow Society. He had heard of their extreme loyalty, their discipline and dedication in their training and their punishments for the slightest failure. Haragan had nearly destroyed his home and almost ruined his father. He'd dropped him into a volcano and left him for dead. He'd tried cheating in the race. But he had also thrown the javelin that had killed the mummy and then helped Zara destroy the Emperor. Zal knew how easy it was to break into the Caliph's palace, but with its talking gates, the Guild school was another matter. Haragan and his friends had woven two carpet fragments together well enough to fly. His carpet was stretched out across the sands now but it had served him very well. The original weavers, whoever they were, would have been proud, Zal thought. He met Haragan's eyes again and spoke.

"I know you tried hard."

Zal couldn't read Haragan's eyes, and the rest of his face was concealed beneath his scarf, but as he was dragged away by the guards, Haragan was smiling. Smiling as bright as the dawn sun. He found his feet, matched his guards' pace and made no attempt to escape. They were taking him to a jail cell. Not to the Shadow headquarters. Not to another humiliating debriefing. Not to more punishment duties. Not to more training and not, after the events of the race, to another possible visit to the Dark Room. They were taking him to a cell, with a proper bed, where the Society would not be able to touch him. He would no longer have to account for himself to people he didn't respect. He didn't have to answer to a society he had never asked to be a part of. Because he was safe with the Citadel Guard. Not only safe, but free. Finally, after all these long years, he was free.

Zal watched him go and then walked back to Zara, Rip and the carpet. Augur and Arna beamed and soon they were all cheering and laughing at their race victory, just as the other contestants began to arrive across the finishing line.

The Thesas and the Auras held a celebratory dinner that night, sitting on the hovering rainbow carpet in Arna's sitting room. A small table with a bouquet of flowers had been placed in the middle of it. In the corner of the room floated a small demon Zara had summoned, and discreetly he played soft music on a seven-stringed violin. The one blight on the day was that Zara's prophecy had been correct: they would never be able to race their carpet again. The Caliph had proclaimed that, despite the tremendous drama, the race had been over far too fast. Carpets of six colours and fewer would still be allowed to compete in the future. Seven colours would be excluded.

"It is fair," said Arna. "You left every other carpet miles behind. They all deserved a chance at winning. But you both achieved so much. Your mothers would be proud of you."

"Ummp," said Zal, swallowing his mouthful. "That's something we have to do. Visit them."

"First thing in the morning," said Zara. "We'll get

flowers first with the prize money. And I agree about the race, Dad. It is fair."

"But that still leaves other options open," said Augur.

"The thread, you mean?" said Arna. Zal and Zara had just finished telling them the full story of their adventure.

"Just so." Augur swallowed his mouthful. "We'll be able to auction it off for a small fortune. Let's face it – we won't be able to keep it a secret for ever. Unless…"

"Unless what?" said Zal.

"The spiders are still down there. If we can go back and capture some of them, we could corner the market for the thread."

"Yes," said Arna. "Zara can use magic on the water dragon and the mummies again, and if you can repeat the six cuts…"

"You bet I can," said Zal. "But there's another reason why we should go back. The bodyguards. The Emperor escaped, but there might still be some of them left down there. They may be Shadows, but they're also ancient Asameedians; our ancestors. They fought for our freedom from slavery and we

225

forgot them. We should tell them the war is over. We should let them rest."

"A very noble thought," said Arna.

"And after that, the shape is the limit," said Zara.

"Yes – sorry?"

"It's something I found when we were flying this one." Zara patted their victorious carpet. "It had a maximum speed because the rectangular shape stopped it from going any faster."

"All carpets have to be rectangular," said Zal.

"I'm not sure any more," said Zara. "I think the rectangle is the only shape that will fly without the transparent thread. But *with* the thread…"

"We could make all sorts of shapes." Zal sat back, imagining it. "Squares, circles, triangles, pentagons…"

"We might not get into the Great Race again," said Augur, "but we could start a new one: the Seven-colour Race. Find out which shape is the best!"

"Well." Arna raised his glass. "The toast is to victory and the future."

"Victory and the future!" they chorused. The glasses chinked.

"Will you perhaps help me weave some of these shapes?" Augur asked Zal.

"Of course," said Zal. "I've got three more years before I'm old enough for the Guard. I might as well make some money in the meantime. And I'll give you those fencing lessons we talked about, Dad."

"I want to teach you to be less wary of magic," said Zara. "If we're going to be racing more, we'll need it. Loads of people saw Haragan's cheats. How many will have got ideas from it?"

"I'd like to learn to parry magic with my sword," said Zal, refilling Zara's glass.

"I'll throw as much combat magic at you as you like," Zara smiled. "It'll be fun."

"Great," said Zal. Then his smile suddenly disappeared and he pointed an angry finger at Zara.

"But I'm still not marrying you!"

Out in the desert, night had fallen. The stars were scattered across the black sky. A lone figure picked and stumbled his way through the sand dunes. A thread reel was in his hands and round it he was winding the single, twisted strand that the Shadow Society's rainbow carpet had been reduced to.

Hani had no fear of discovery. Shar and Dari had been grabbed by the Citadel Guard as soon as they had staggered through the city gates. Other Shadows were being arrested left, right and centre. Their Leader was rumoured to have fled the city. None of them would have the time to come looking for their carpet.

His carpet now.

He had come last this year. His shoddily woven indigo carpet, that he really should have put more effort into enchanting, had been the last one to skim across the line. No one had noticed. All had been too busy talking about the Thesas'. But he couldn't begrudge Zara Aura: she deserved it for all the other times she had been beaten by Haragan.

But next year would be different. The Shadow carpet was his carpet now. He would re-weave it, and he'd do a much better job than they had. Seven-colour carpets were now banned, but that didn't mean the secret couldn't be used in a six-colour. Who knew to what effect? He would find the secret they hadn't bothered to look for. And then...

Yes. Next year would be different. The race, the races, would be spectacular.

All is not well in the crumbling castle high above
the mountain village of Fracture. The sorceress Lady
Lamorna has her heart set on a new robe. A very
expensive new robe. To get the cash she will stop at
nothing, including kidnapping, blackmail and more
than a little black magic. But she reckons without
the heroic Gracie Gillypot, not to mention a gallant
if rather scruffy prince, two chatty bats, the wickedest
stepsister ever, a troll with a grudge – and some very
Ancient Crones.

BY VIVIAN FRENCH

When she was ten years old, Katrina Picket woke Merlin. It was quite by accident – she'd had no intention of doing any such thing. But it was fortunate for everyone in England that she did. They didn't know, of course. The whole thing had to be hushed up. Most people thought it was a particularly inventive party for the Queen's jubilee. And as for the dragon and the exploding fireball – they were explained away as impressive special effects. But Katrina, and the Prime Minister, knew different...

BY TANYA LANDMAN

Shanghai, 1920: while on board the *Expedient*, Doug and Becca MacKenzie await news of their missing parents ... and stumble across a far greater mystery.

England, 2002: Joshua Mowll inherits a remarkable archive of documents and painstakingly pieces together the extraordinary events that took place over eighty years earlier.

This is the story of a mysterious Guild striving to protect an ancient secret; the story of two young people caught up in an astonishing adventure ... with far-reaching consequences for the whole world.

BY JOSHUA MOWLL

Lost and alone, a young cat called Mati seeks accept-
ance into a community of street cats at Cressida
Lock. But Mati is no ordinary cat ... and Mithos, the
mysterious assassin on his trail, knows it. To defeat
his enemies, Mati must unlock the secret of his true
identity. In doing so, he must learn to harness an
ancient feline power – a power so deadly that it
threatens to destroy not only his friends but every cat
on earth...

BY INBALI ISERLES

Patricia: "Warren Buffett's Wisdom for Powerful Women." In: *Fortune*, 6 October 2010. See: http://fortune.com/2010/10/06/warren-buffetts-wisdom-for-powerful-women/ (accessed on 11 July 2017).

50. *Sturgeon's Law*

The original quotation from Ted Sturgeon: "When people talk about the mystery novel, they mention *The Maltese Falcon* and *The Big Sleep*. When they talk about the western, they say there's *The Way West* and *Shane*. But when they talk about science fiction, they call it 'that Buck Rogers stuff,' and they say 'ninety percent of science fiction is crud.' Well, they're right. Ninety percent of science fiction is crud. But then ninety percent of everything is crud, and it's the ten percent that isn't crud that is important, and the ten percent of science fiction that isn't crud is as good as or better than anything being written anywhere." (Dennett, Daniel: *Intuition Pumps and Other Tools for Thinking*, W. W. Norton, 2013, E-Book Location 639).

Daniel Dennett: "90 percent of everything is crap. That is true, whether you are talking about physics, chemistry, evolutionary psychology, sociology, medicine—you name it—rock music, country western. 90 percent of everything is crap." See: https://en.wikipedia.org/wiki/Sturgeon percent27s_law#cite_ref-5 (accessed on 11 July 2017).

Harry Frankfurt, professor of philosophy at Princeton University, published a bestseller a few years back that was snappily titled *On Bullshit*. (Frankfurt, Harry G.: *On Bullshit*, Princeton University Press, 2005, p. 61.) In the book he demonstrates that lies aren't the main enemy of truth; *bullshit* is. Frankfurt defines bullshit as speech devoid of content that nonetheless pretends to be relevant, but I think the definition can usefully be broadened. *Bullshit* is the ninety percent that *Sturgeon's law* dictates is irrelevant—no matter whether you're talking about books, fashion trends or lifestyles.

The world can stay irrational longer than you can stay sane. I came up with this phrase as a counterpart to *Sturgeon's law*. It's an adaptation of a quotation from John Maynard Keynes: "The market can stay irrational longer than you can stay solvent." See: https://www.maynardkeyncs.org/keynes-the-speculator.html (accessed on 11 July 2017).

On Benjamin Graham's idea about *Mr. Market* see: https://en.wikipedia.org/wiki/Mr._Market (accessed on 11 July 2017).

51. In Praise of Modesty

Think about how important you would have had to be in order to be invited to the official opening ceremonies of the Eiffel Tower (complete with a gourmet banquet) in 1889, the Taj Mahal in 1648 or the Great Pyramid of Giza in 2581 B.C. Khufu himself invited you! You sit there on the stage, gazing at the newly constructed pyramid as slaves waft a warm desert breeze into your face, hoping that the ceremony—the dances, the speeches, the dull parade of soldiers—will soon be over and you can move on to the "relaxing part." How important you must have felt! How baselessly important.

Here's a nice example of modesty and rationality: the American general George Marshall (after whom the Marshall Plan to help rebuild Europe was named) had to sit for an official portrait, as was customary in those days. "After appearing many times and patiently honoring the requests, Marshall was finally informed by the painter that he was finished and free to go. Marshall stood up and began to leave. 'Don't you want to see the painting?' the artist asked. 'No, thank you,' Marshall said respectfully and left." (Holiday, Ryan: *Ego Is the Enemy,* Portfolio, 2016, E-Book Location 1628.) "Who has time to look at a picture of himself? What's the point?" (ibid., E-Book Location 1634.)

I described the *self-serving bias* and *overconfidence* in another book. Dobelli, Rolf: *The Art of Thinking Clearly,* HarperCollins Publishers, 2012, pp. 134–136 and pp. 43–45.)

52. Inner Success

"By linking prestige and esteem to particular activities or accomplishments, a culture can direct many people to devote their energies in those directions. It is no accident that in small societies struggling for survival, prestige comes with bringing in large amounts of protein (hunting) or defeating the most dangerous enemies (fighting). By the same token, the prestige of motherhood probably rises and falls with the society's need to increase population, and the prestige of entertainers rises and falls with how much time and money the population can devote to leisure activities." (Baumeister, Roy: *The Cultural Animal,* Oxford University Press, 2005, p. 146.)

Why are there lists of the richest people but not lists of the most satisfied people? Well, there are life satisfaction rankings, but only on a national rather than individual level. The OECD regularly publishes a superbly compiled ranking—Norway and Switzerland have been vying for the top spot for years. See: http://www.oecdbetterlifeindex.org (accessed on 12 July 2017).

"Growth is needed to maintain social cohesion. The prospect of improvements in living standards, however remote, limits pressure for wealth redistribution. As Henry Wallick, a former Governor of the U.S. Federal Reserve, accurately diagnosed: 'So long as there is growth there is hope, and that makes large income differential tolerable.'" (Das, Satyajit: "A World Without Growth?" In: Brockman, *What Should We Be Worried About?*, Harper Perennial, 2014, p. 110.)

Warren Buffett: "If I'd been born thousands of years ago I'd be some animal's lunch because I can't run very fast or climb trees. So there's so much chance in how we enter the world." See: http://www.businessin sider.com/warren-buffett-nails-it-on-the-importance-of-luck-in-life -2013-10 (accessed on 11 July 2017).

John Wooden: "Success is peace of mind, which is a direct result of self-satisfaction in knowing you made the effort to do your best to become the best that you are capable of becoming." (Wooden, John: *The Difference Between Winning and Succeeding,* TED-Talk, 2009. See: https://www.youtube.com/watch?v=0MM-psvqiG8 (time: 3:00).

You don't have to be the richest person in the cemetery; be the most inwardly successful person in the here and now. Adapted from a quotation from John Spears: "You don't have to be the richest guy in the cemetery." (Green, William; O'Brian, Michael: *The Great Minds of Investing,* Finanzbuch Verlag, 2015, p. 72.)

John Wooden: "Make each day your masterpiece." See: https://en.wiki pedia.org/wiki/John_Wooden#cite_note-94 (accessed on 11 July 2017).

Afterword

Richard Feynman: "You can know the name of a bird in all the languages of the world, but when you're finished, you'll know absolutely nothing whatever about the bird...So let's look at the bird and see what it's doing—that's what counts. I learned very early the difference between knowing the name of something and knowing something." See: https://www.youtube.com/watch?v=ga_7j72Cvlc and http://www .quotationspage.com/quote/26933.html (accessed on 11 July 2017).

One of the best definitions I know of the *good life* comes from Epictetus, the Stoic: "A life that flows gently and easily." (Epictetus, *Discourses*, 1.4). Another definition came to me over lunch with a friend, an entrepreneur who had built up a fortune of several hundred million. It was summer. We were sitting outside. The pub had metal tables that had been repainted several times, our shoes crunched on the gravel, and we had to be careful that no wasps had crawled over the rims of our glasses when we lifted our ice tea to our lips. We talked mostly about my work—plans for this book—and his: investment strategies, financial interests, asset management, issues with donations, problems with employees, drivers, servants, maintenance on his private jet and, on top of this, his time-consuming positions on various boards of directors, whose prestigious membership he had earned not merely because of his wealth. Suddenly the words tumbled from my lips: "Why, my dear friend, do you do it all? If I had all your millions, I'd spend my time doing nothing but reading, thinking and writing." It wasn't until I was on the way home that I realized, oddly startled, that that's exactly what I do. So that would be a definition of the *good life*: somebody hands you a few million, and you don't change anything at all.